DECRYPTION
THE GENESIS MACHINE
BOOK 2

K. J. GILLENWATER

Decryption

Cover art by Miblart

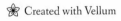 Created with Vellum

CHAPTER 1

1498. Val Camonica, Northern Italy.

RISA SQUEEZED her son's hand. Crouching in the bushes on the edge of the woods in the dark would frighten any little boy. Being chased by a fearful mob multiplied that feeling times ten, times one hundred.

One times ten is ten.

Two times ten is twenty.

Three times ten is thirty.

Her mind latched on to the things that comforted her: numbers, logic, science.

Things a woman shouldn't know.

Things a woman could be killed for.

Things that not only she could be killed for, but her child. Her innocent child. It was as if an invisible hand squeezed her heart.

She could not lose her son to this mob of witch hunters.

Voices shouted nearby. Lantern light shot through the dark. Dozens of lanterns.

They'd never make it.

How much further to go?

As she pushed through the shrubs, she dragged her exhausted child with her.

"Mama," he wailed.

She clamped a hand over his mouth. *"Tranquillo,* little one." She knelt on the soft grass and gathered him in her arms. "We are almost there. I need you to be very brave for me. Can you do that?"

The boy nodded and clutched her tightly around the neck. *"Ho paura,* Mama."

She whispered into his blond hair, "I know, *caro."* She stood and held his hand tightly. "Come, we're almost there, and then we'll be safe. I promise. *Promesso."*

But she didn't know if her promise would come to fruition. She'd only finished crafting the machines in the last few days. The first one had been an abject failure. It had turned into a pile of green mush within moments. The formula was not quite the same as she'd remembered.

Her experiments had caught the notice of the wrong people. Not the friendly nuns who'd taken her in—a lost, pregnant woman with no husband. But the religious fanatics who increasingly feared the dark arts and blamed innocent women as the perpetrators. In the last year, their fears reached a fever pitch, and focus turned toward the *donna strana* at the nunnery.

Who was she? Where had she come from? Why did she speak a foreign tongue? Why was she seen late at night in the woods near the river? Was her child a child of the devil?

Although the nuns had welcomed her into their community years ago, they'd questioned her strange clothing and mysterious arrival. But when they'd learned of her ability to read and write, they'd found her quite useful. So despite the suspicions of those outside the cloister, they had given her very much needed sanctuary. For within her mind resided the secret to returning to her life and the father of her child.

"*Lei è andata così!*" one of her accusers bellowed.

They were mere steps behind her and her son. The pounding of her heart filled her ears until she could hear nothing else. Branches scratched at her face and tore at her rough woolen dress and the kirtle underneath.

Ahead, she saw the machines lurking in a copse of trees, blending in with their green leaves. She dropped her son's hand, leaving him in a marshy meadow dotted with moonlight, and raced toward them. In the soft hull she pressed a hidden button to expose a hatch.

"Come, *caro*, come. You must get inside." Risa beckoned her child forward.

The rumble of the mob crashing through the woods made her breath hitch in her throat. She'd seen what they'd done to others accused of being witches: torture, burning, horrible things. But a child? What would they do to an innocent child? The horror was too much for her mind.

"*Non voglio,*" he said, planting his feet. "No."

There was no time to waste. No time to cajole. Her voice grew sharp, and she hated herself for it. "Inside. *Ora!*" She grabbed him by the arm and dragged him into the machine.

He was afraid of the dark, and the machine appeared to be a black hole.

"No, Mama! No!" Her son fought against her.

"Sit." She shoved him into the single seat inside the machine and strapped him in. The soft flexible safety harness melded with it as if it had always been a part of it.

"Mama!" The boy cried and struggled in the tight restraint.

She wished she'd had time to explain to him what was happening, where he was going, and why. Risa thought she would have had more time. In fact, she wasn't even sure the machines would function properly. The original machine she'd arrived in had failed miserably. She was so off course and had no idea why. A fault of design? A bad program?

"*Eccola!*" the mob entered into the meadow. "*E anche il suo bambino diavolo!*"

"Lord help us," she whispered. She'd never let them take her son. Never.

She fiddled with the controls and set it as best she could remember. It had been years since she'd been inside a machine. Would Byron be on the other side waiting for his son? Would someone make sure he was reunited with his father?

No time to waste. She had no choice. She entered the last of the data.

"I will see you there, my son. Do not fear." She touched his tear-stained cheek and then kissed him on the forehead. "*Ti amo figlio mio.*"

Rough hands pulled her out of the machine.

The boy cried and struggled in the seat. "Mama!"

"My son!" she cried. These animals might kill her, but they would not touch her child.

She raged against the arms that held her. Stinking, dirty, soulless humans. The same kind of men who'd destroyed her world. The same kind of men who'd forced her to flee for her life and her child's life once before. She screamed and bit at her captors' hands. Flailing like a wild cat, she broke free and lunged for the shell of the machine. The meat of her palm pressed the hidden button a second time.

As the hatch closed, a wave of relief filled her. He would be safe. No matter what happened to her, he would be safe.

A heavy object landed with a crack on her skull. Warm blood poured out and ran down her face. It was too late. The other machine would remain unused and disintegrate in the next heavy downpour. But as she lost consciousness and fell into the arms of the men who surrounded her, she smiled as the machine began to spin and spin and spin. Faster and faster until it turned into a blur of motion and green.

"My son," she whispered one last time.

The machine disappeared, and the men fell back in fear.

CHAPTER 2

THE CHILD CLUNG so tightly to her neck, Charlie thought she might go under. Although she didn't want to frighten the poor thing even more, she plunged underwater. The shock of the action forced the child to release his grip.

She surfaced, sputtering. Then she scooped under the dark water, found the boy, and hauled him up. After snaking an arm across his chest, she snugged him to her side.

"You're going to be all right." Did the boy even understand her? Where did he come from? Why was he in the pod all alone? "I've got you."

With a strong side stroke, Charlie towed the child back to shore. After the dunking he received, he calmed down and laid limply in the water—too scared or too tired to fight her.

The pod's green glow flickered out as it sank further into the river. The open hatch sped up the process. As her feet hit the bottom near the shoreline, the final curve of the pod disappeared into the black water. Any opportunity to study it was lost to the river and the dark.

"Cutter!" Demarco rushed toward her, gun in hand. "Are you all right?"

She emerged from the water with the small child on her hip. Her legs trembled, and her whole body shivered. "Didn't think the water would be so cold."

The special agent reeled back at the sight of the boy. His forehead wrinkled. "Who's that?"

"Put that away." She pointed at the gun. "You're scaring him."

The boy's rounded eyes reminded her of the Starry Night Owl painting she'd abandoned in Fairfax.

"I don't understand." Demarco's shoulders slumped. He looked out over the river. "I saw you swim to the pod...and then...but how—?"

Charlie reached his position on the shore. "This little guy was inside the pod all by himself." The boy hid his face in her neck, and a maternal feeling awoke inside her. She wrapped an arm across his thin back in an act of comfort. "I hope the commander shows up soon. What the hell is going on here?"

"It can't be." Demarco's mouth slackened, and he backed away. "It's impossible. I don't understand."

"Where are you going? This boy needs our help." How could Demarco fail to help a little boy so clearly in distress? "Do you have a blanket in your car? We're freezing."

Her scolding snapped him out of it. "Yes, wait, I think I do. Stay there. I'll be right back."

He trotted toward the parked vehicle.

"*Dov'è mia madre?*" asked the child in a whisper.

Without even thinking, Charlie replied, "*Non lo so, ma la troveremo.*" She hugged him tight. "We will find your mother, I promise."

She found a weathered Adirondack chair and huddled with the boy in her lap. His tunic felt rough under her fingers and appeared to be hand sewn. He had deep brown eyes and a thin face, which made him appear malnourished. As they rested there, she combed her fingers through his long locks in a soothing gesture.

"Looks like you made a new friend, Petty Officer." Commander Orr arrived and handed her a silver emergency blanket.

"Am I happy to see you, sir. Thank you." She wrapped the boy in it and set him in the chair. "*Aspetta qui.*"

"No!" The child reached for her.

She disentangled her arm from his grasp. "I left my clothes over there, sir." The sleeveless blouse she'd chosen to wear provided little cover, and now that she'd recovered some from the shock of what had happened, she wanted to be a little more presentable before the rest of the team arrived.

The commander nodded. "Go ahead. I can take care of the little tyke." He kept his gaze on the child and ignored her state of undress.

"Let me grab your clothes," Demarco offered. "Here, you can put this on." He handed her a plaid shirt. "From my go-bag."

The wind picked up and blew against her naked legs. "Thank you." She slipped into the shirt, which covered her to mid-thigh.

"So Demarco told me the boy was inside the pod? Is that correct?" The commander tucked the blanket around the child who seemed fascinated by its shiny, silver exterior.

"I saw the pod in the river and swam out to it. I thought if it had just landed there could be a chance a live alien might be inside." She relived the moment the boy had appeared in the open hatch. "Instead, it was him." She rubbed her temples. "I don't understand, sir. I thought we were seeking aliens and alien tech. But he's no alien. He's a human boy."

"I'm trying to wrap my mind around it, too, Petty Officer," said the commander. "Everything we've learned so far led us to believe these were unidentified objects—things not of this world. The samples we've collected, the writing—"

"Here." Demarco returned with her shoes and jeans. His demeanor had cooled.

"Thanks." She quickly donned her pants and slipped on her shoes.

The boy, fascinated, watched her dress.

"You said something to him earlier...what language was that?" Demarco asked.

"When you went to your car he asked me, 'Dov'è mia madre.' It's Italian for 'Where's my mother.'"

"You know Russian and Italian?" Commander Orr asked.

"I was a linguistics major, so I learned a little bit of everything, really."

The commander put his hands on his hips. "So what is an Italian boy doing in an alien pod in the middle of the Occoquan River?"

———

"The pod. It's gone," Lieutenant Kellerman said as he approached the rest of the team unaware of the passenger they tended to. "Dammit. I thought this time we'd collect some really good samples."

"We found something better than the pod," Charlie said, kneeling next to the boy. She ruffled his drying hair. "This little bugger."

Orr had found a small tin of mints in his pocket and had handed it to the child, who liked to slide the box open and closed more than he liked the mints inside. He leaned his head against Charlie's leg as she stood next to the chair.

Kellerman stopped dead in his tracks. "Someone going to explain what's going on?"

"I'd love to hear the story, too," Chief Ricard said, the next of the team to arrive. "I left my wife stranded at the movies. She practically smacked me when I told her I had to leave. I don't see a pod." He threw up his hands. "Shit. Was it a false alarm?"

Demarco paced on the rocky shore.

Why did he seem so aggravated? The discovery of the boy opened up a whole new track of exploration.

"Petty Officer Cutter, can you please tell everyone what happened? Then we can decide what our next steps should be. Theories. Ideas. I'll take any of it."

"Theories?" Cole Kellerman raised a brow. "What happened?"

"When Demarco and I arrived—"

"Wait," interrupted Ricard, "you and Demarco came together?" He shifted his gaze from Charlie to the special agent. "I think I'd rather hear that story first."

"Chief, that's a most inappropriate comment," Orr scolded. "Please, Petty Officer, continue."

Great. The last thing she needed was gossip going around the office about her and Demarco. Ugh. "As I was saying, we reached the end of the road, and I could see a pod glowing in the distance. Quite deep in the water at the mouth of the bay." She pointed in the direction of the pod location. "So I swam for it."

"Wow." Kellerman's eyes widened and his mouth went slack.

"She's a hot dog in the pool," the commander added. "Saw it for myself."

Charlie cleared her throat. "Anyway, I swam out there thinking an alien could be inside and might need help. A hatch opened and out he came." She knelt beside the boy.

The child pulled his attention away from the tin of mints and smiled at her. *"Grazie, signora."*

"Wait a second." The chief gave his head a shake. "You're telling me this kid—" He pointed at the little boy dwarfed by the large chair. "—came out of a pod?"

For a few beats no one spoke.

He walked over to the commander. "You've got to be shitting me if you believe this story, sir."

Charlie stood. "Hey, are you calling me a liar?" She crossed to the two men. "That boy was inside the pod. Whatever we are dealing with here, it's not aliens. That's what I know. He's a human boy inside a pod. Whoever told you that these things were from outer space is wrong. Dead wrong. The whole thing didn't make a lot of sense to me from the beginning, but I was brought on the team to do a job."

Chief Ricard met her with equal emotion. "So you're telling me this whole time you knew it wasn't aliens, but never said anything? You've been with A Group for a week, and now you think you have all the answers." He stepped between her and Orr to block the commander's view of Cutter. "She's lying to you, sir. I don't know what her angle is, but she's lying. We've been on this shit since last year, and some of the data we have defies explanation. This has to be alien tech...maybe she wants some sort of attention or something. I don't get it. But I don't believe one word of it."

Kellerman approached and stood abreast of Charlie. "I believe her." He gave her a reassuring smile.

"Thanks, Cole."

"Does it really matter if you believe her or not, Chief?" Kellerman said. "The pod sank. There's nothing to collect. All we have is Petty Officer Cutter's story and a child with no parents. Shouldn't we at least give Dr. Stern a call and ask her to meet us at the office? The boy is the only evidence we have to test."

Charlie felt a tug on her pants. She looked down, and the boy had left the chair. The emergency blanket twisted around his small body. "*Signora?*"

Charlie threw a harsh gaze at the scowling chief and knelt so she would be at the boy's eye level. "*Sí?*"

"Where's Mama?" he said in perfect unaccented English.

Commander Orr jerked his head back. "Yes, I'll give Dr. Stern a call." He pulled out his cell. "Maybe she'll know what we're dealing with here." He stared mystified at the bilingual boy who'd landed in their care and then wandered away from the group to talk to the doctor.

"Did he just speak in English?" Demarco rejoined the group.

Guess he'd played out his temper tantrum by the river and came back to his senses. Would've been nice if he'd backed up her story instead of letting the chief beat her up.

"Yes, he did." Charlie hugged the thin child to her side.

Chief Ricard followed Orr. After implying some kind of unseemly relationship between Demarco and Charlie, he clearly was avoiding a confrontation with the special agent. Plus, he seemed to have no interest in the child.

The mysterious boy gave her a shy smile. "You are pretty. *Carina*. Like Mama." He touched her hair with his tiny fingers.

Her heart warmed, and she couldn't help but grab his little hand in hers and kiss the back of it. "Thank you."

The boy laughed and quickly tucked his hand inside the emergency blanket, as if she'd tickled him.

"What's your name? My name is Charlie." She touched her chest with her palm.

"Armas," he said, pounding his little chest in response. "*Mi chiamo Armas.*"

Demarco noticeably stiffened.

Odd.

"Very pleased to meet you, Armas," Kellerman said, leaning down to shake the boy's hand in a very formal fashion. "My name is Cole."

Armas laughed and did a little dance as he shook the lieutenant's hand in an exaggerated fashion.

"We need to find his parents," Demarco said, his expression unreadable.

"Don't tell me you think I'm lying, too." What a bastard. He'd witnessed practically the whole rescue, and instead of supporting her story, he wanted to agree with Chief Ricard's view?

"Until Dr. Stern can examine him and do some tests, I think we can agree we have no idea where this boy came from or who he belongs to."

Kellerman let out a snort. "You're just as bad as the chief. We all know a pod landed here. We have the radar signal to prove it. Did you see a pod or didn't you?"

"I did," admitted Demarco.

Kellerman took a step toward the special agent. "Did you see her swim out there and come back with the boy?"

"Yes, I saw her swim out and then return with the child in her arms." He let out a sigh. "Against my orders, by the way."

Charlie scooped up Armas and held him close. He looped an arm around her neck as if he'd done it a million times before. "Why don't you ask Armas where he came from? Wouldn't that settle it for you?"

Demarco crossed his arms. "He's maybe four years old. He probably can't even tell us what cartoon he watched this morning."

How infuriating that Mr. Security himself couldn't admit what he saw with his own eyes. Armas had come out of the pod.

"Team!" Commander Orr interrupted the dispute. "Dr. Stern will meet us at our office with the necessary equipment for the tests she wants to run. Can someone please get in touch with Stormy and let her know the change of plans?"

Kellerman tapped on his phone. "On it, sir."

Chief already was heading to his vehicle in the cul-de-sac.

Thank God she didn't have to hear his blathering anymore. Dr. Stern would prove to him the truth of her story.

"Agent Demarco, you and Petty Officer Cutter take the boy with you." He smiled at Armas. "He seems to have taken a shine to our newest team member."

Drive back with Demarco? Crap. "Sir, couldn't I go with Kellerman?"

The special agent tilted his chin down and frowned.

"Why, do you have a problem with Demarco?" His placed his hands on his hips.

That had been a mistake.

"No, sir," she said. "That's fine with me. No problem at all."

Orr turned to the special agent. "And you?"

"No problem, sir."

"Perfect. We're on the same page then. See you at HQ." The commander turned on his heel and crunched down the gravel path to his vehicle.

"You trying to get me in trouble?" Demarco said in a harsh whisper.

"You did it to yourself," Charlie said as she headed toward the Landcruiser. She adjusted the young boy on her hip. "Armas, let's find out where you came from. How does that sound? *Buona idea?*"

"*Si,*" Armas said.

Demarco jogged to catch up to the two of them. "You are being unreasonable."

"Am I?" Charlie focused her attention on the road ahead.

"We don't know a thing about this boy."

"Armas. His name is Armas."

"Armas!" The boy clapped his hands together.

The special agent let out a sigh. "I know his name."

She paused at the top of the rise near the curb and faced him. "I thought we had decided to work together."

"We did."

"Working together means trusting your partner." Did he already forget? "When we arrived, you made me wait in the car."

"Right. It was too dangerous—"

"We were the first people on the scene." She touched the boy's bare knee, exposed by the short tunic. "We almost lost our opportunity to save little Armas."

"What if it had been a full-grown man in that pod?" He took in her blank expression. Then he closed his eyes and pinched his nose.

"I don't think I did anything wrong here. We didn't know what we were walking into."

"Second, when the chief accused me of making up a story, where were you? Pacing the beach in your own little world. You hung me out to dry." Couldn't he see how he'd undermined her back there? "Not only that, you sided with him. After witnessing the whole thing for yourself."

"I didn't see everything," he mumbled.

"You saw enough." She jutted out her hip to hold the weight of the boy more comfortably. "Look, let's go back to the office, do what we need to do, and call it a night. I'm tired."

"Excellent idea."

In silence they walked side-by-side to the Landcruiser. The rest of the crew had already left.

As they approached the vehicle, Armas gasped. "*Cos'è?*"

"What?" Demarco asked. "What did he say?"

"*Cos'è quella cosa*, Charlie?" Armas struggled in her arms. "Down, down."

She set him on the pavement. "He wants to know what that is."

"What?" Demarco asked.

Armas ran up to the Landcruiser and pounded on the bumper "*Cos'è quella cosa*, Charlie? *Cos'è quella cosa?*"

"Your car." Charlie couldn't keep the shock out of her voice.

Where did this boy come from?

CHAPTER 3

ARMAS RAN a hand along the smooth side of Demarco's Landcruiser. "Car," he said. His eyes rounded, and his little mouth formed an 'o.'

The special agent hung back, frowned, and tilted his head to one side.

Charlie approached the boy who touched every surface he could reach: the bumper, the door, the handle, the side view mirror. "Yes, it's called a car. We go places in it."

Armas paused and faced her. "Go?"

"*Andiamo.*" Charlie touched the hood of the Toyota. "*Andiamo in macchina.* We go in the car."

"*Macchina?*" He pressed his elbows into his sides and curved his shoulders inward. "*Non voglio andare in macchina.*"

"What's wrong with him?" Demarco's eyes narrowed.

"Hey, hey, it's okay." Charlie knelt and gave the trembling boy a hug. "You don't need to be scared. We'll take care of you. *Ci prenderemo cura di te.*"

Armas clung to her neck and hid his face.

"He's terrified," Charlie said, glancing at the special agent.

"Well, he's going to have to get over it." Demarco placed his hands on his hips. "This is how we take him back to the office. He needs to get in the rig."

Why did Demarco have to be so impatient? Armas had plopped down, alone, in a pod that came from who knows where. The plummet to Earth must have been frightening to a boy so young.

"Just relax," she said to Demarco. The special agent likely scared Armas even more with his harsh tone. "I'll convince him. Give me a little bit of time, would you?"

"Fine." Demarco gave both woman and boy a wide berth as he passed in front of the vehicle and unlocked the driver's side door. "I'll give you five minutes before I make him get in."

What an emotionless jerk. No sympathy for a small child? Everything was about him all the time.

Gently, she held Armas by the shoulders and tipped up his chin. "Don't be afraid. I'll sit with you. *Mi siederò con te.* I will make sure you are safe."

His wide brown eyes shone with tears. "Charlie, you will sit with me?" He cracked a broad smile revealing a missing tooth in the bottom front row of teeth.

"Yes. I will sit right next to you." She squeezed his narrow shoulders. "I think you might like it."

Armas looked up at the Landcruiser and touched its painted exterior once more. "We go in the car."

"That's right." Charlie stood and locked eyes with Demarco who sat behind the wheel. She gave him a little nod.

"How? How do we go in the car?" Armas pushed against the side panel with all his might.

"Not like that, Armas." She caught one of his hands and pulled him away. If the boy left a dent in his classic Toyota, Demarco would kill her. "Here."

Charlie pulled the handle on the door to the back seat and opened it. The child gasped.

She scooped him up and placed him on the black vinyl seats.

Immediately, Armas stood up in his sandy, muddy bare feet and marred the clean vinyl. "Go, car, go!"

"Sit down." Demarco turned his body half way around to growl at him.

The boy's lower lip trembled.

"It's all right, Armas. Come here." She grabbed the boy and sat him in her lap. "Let's sit down, and you can look out the window. *Finestra.*"

She shot Demarco what she hoped was a look of death.

He shrugged and started the engine.

The boy trembled at the loud noise.

Charlie whispered soothing words in his ear in Italian, and his body relaxed.

By the time they'd reached the end of the cul-de-sac, Armas was excitedly pointing at random lights glowing in the yards of each house they passed.

"*La luce!*"

If Armas marveled at a car and electric lights, what would he think when they arrived in D.C.?

"*Gli uomini con le luci stanno arrivando,*" the boy whispered in her ear.

"*Gli uomini?*" she asked. "What men?"

"The men who hurt my mama. They had many lights." Armas balled up in her lap. "*Dov'è mia madre?*

Distressed by the child's deep seated fear, Charlie soothed him by running her hand across his head. "We will find her, Armas. I promise you."

But as Demarco drove them ever closer to D.C. Charlie wondered about her promise. After what she'd seen and experienced tonight, doubts set in about being able to locate the child's parents. Little Armas seemed to be a boy with no past, no home, and no knowledge of the world he'd landed in. How very strange.

———

"Where is this child?" Dr. Stern asked as soon as Charlie and Demarco entered the office.

"Shh." Charlie carried the sleeping boy in her arms. He'd fallen into a deep sleep about ten minutes into their trip. Exhausted from everything probably. "He's asleep."

Stormy rushed around the cubicle walls to meet them. "The commander told us you found a child in the pod." She scanned Armas from head to bare feet, and her face softened. "He's so young."

No surprise the young mother would have instant sympathy. The rest of the team stood back, as if Armas had a communicable disease.

Her mind raced.

Wait, what if he did? What if he brought some kind of virus or contaminant with him?

Too late for her now. She'd been exposed to anything he may have brought with him.

Dr. Stern approached on cat feet. "He really came out of the pod?" Her slender fingers stopped centimeters short of touching the boy's hair.

"Yes. Despite what some may have told you." Charlie didn't even want to look at Chief Ricard right now, but she hoped he heard her words.

"His clothes," the doctor said. "He was wearing this?"

"Yes, I'm not sure what it's made of, but it looks hand sewn."

Dr. Stern carefully fingered the hem of the garment. "Homespun wool. Undyed." She nodded. "Primitive."

"I didn't know you knew so much about fabrics."

"In another life, I used to sew." She let go of the tunic. "When I had time."

Stormy hovered. "I think my pea coat is hanging in the closet. Maybe we can make a little bed for him in the conference room?"

Charlie nodded. Who knew a little boy could be so heavy?

"Seems cruel to wake him up just so I can poke and prod him," said Dr. Stern. "Maybe in the morning?"

"We need those samples analyzed immediately," Commander Orr said.

"I'll set up everything here." Dr. Stern sat a hard case of equipment on an empty desk.

Stormy made her way to the conference room with her pea coat retrieved from the coat closet next to the copy machine.

Demarco stood by the commander. "He had no idea what a car was, electric lights, and you should've seen him when we reached the highway."

Chief Ricard snorted. "Ridiculous. Look, you don't need me here. Until the doctor does her exam and has some results, I think my job is done." He yawned. " Nancy's pissed. I'd rather be asleep at home right now."

Orr swept an invisible fleck of lint off the sleeve of his blue Henley shirt. "Fine, Chief. Go." He checked his watch. "But I want you back here at 0800."

"On a Sunday?" Ricard blinked rapidly. "For this kid?"

"If you'd let me finish my thought, Chief Ricard, perhaps you'd understand," Orr intoned.

Chief's face turned redder than normal.

"I'd like for you to review the radar signature of this latest pod. When did it appear? How long was it tracked? From which direction? Altitude?" The commander ticked off on his fingers. "Since we don't have a pod to analyze, we use the data we have. Kellerman will help you."

"Where is Kellerman?" Ricard crossed his arms.

"He probably stopped for gas," Orr said. "So, tomorrow at 0800? I'll text the lieutenant."

"Yes, sir." Chief turned on his heel and headed to the door. "Nancy isn't going to like this," he muttered on the way past Charlie.

"Demarco," the commander said. "You can help Dr. Stern with her sample collection."

"Can't he rest for a little while?" Charlie held the sleeping boy just outside the conference room.

Orr worried his lip for a few seconds. "Fine. Thirty minutes. Then, we need to wake him."

"Okay." Charlie looked to Demarco. "Could you bring me my sweater? It's on the back on my chair. Since we don't have a blanket—"

"No problem." The special agent scooped up her sweater and brought it to her. "Here." He peered down at Armas. "All tuckered out."

From distant to concerned. Demarco made zero sense sometimes. "I can't even imagine what this little guy's been through."

As she carried him into the dark conference room where Stormy had crafted a bed out of her coat, Demarco leaned against the door frame. "I hope tomorrow he can answer our questions, once he's settled and rested."

Charlie lay the boy on the coat and covered him with her sweater. He sighed and rolled onto his side.

As she watched the boy sleep, the evening played out in her mind. His strange arrival, his lack of knowledge about modern things, and his clothing. Somewhere in the Voynich manuscript there had to be answers. A four-year-old boy could only explain so much.

"Yes," she said. "Tomorrow."

———

"Mama!"

Stormy and Charlie rushed into the conference room. Armas had only managed to sleep for twenty minutes.

Stormy flipped on the lights.

The boy screamed.

Armas crawled under the conference table.

"The lights, turn off the lights." Maybe Chief Ricard didn't believe her and Demarco, but Armas seemed to lack knowledge of the most regular of things—like electricity and lights.

"I'm sorry." Stormy plunged the room into darkness once more. "The poor little thing had a nightmare."

Charlie got down on her hands and knees. "Your mother isn't here, baby."

The boy rubbed at his eyes. "Where's Mama?"

She sat back on her heels. "Come here, Armas." Oh, that face. So awful. How could she help him in such an impossible situation?

He crawled toward her and climbed in her lap. "Charlie, *ho paura*."

"I know you're scared, but I'm here." She turned so Armas could see Stormy's shadowed figure standing behind them. "Stormy is here. We all want to help you."

He sniffed a few times and then rested his head on her shoulder.

"Maybe I should ask Dr. Stern to come in?" Stormy asked.

Charlie nodded. "Might as well. Then we can figure out what the next steps are. He can't live in the office."

"Right." Stormy cleared her throat and played with a fine gold chain around her neck. "Let me go round up Dr. Stern."

Charlie rearranged herself so she sat cross legged on the floor and lifted Armas into a more forward-facing position. "*La dottoressa vuole vederti.*"

"*Dottoressa?*"

"Yes, the doctor. Dr. Stern." She leaned forward and whispered in his ear. "She's very nice."

Abigail Stern entered the room with Stormy right behind her. "I hear someone is awake." She focused her gaze on Charlie. "Stormy said he speaks English."

"Yes." Charlie gave the boy a gentle squeeze. "Although he seems to prefer Italian."

"All right." The doctor opened her case and took out small plastic baggies and a pair of scissors. "I'd like to take some samples of his clothing: the fabric, the stitching. Once we have something else for him to wear, we can analyze the entire piece, but a small sample should get the ball rolling."

Armas stared at the shiny scissors.

"It's a little dark in here," Dr. Stern said. "Can we bring him closer to the doorway? Stormy said he was afraid of the lights, but it will be hard to take my samples without a little more light."

Charlie stood the boy up and then wriggled her way to the door.

Armas laughed at her unusual maneuver.

Score one for Auntie Charlie.

Dr. Stern knelt and quickly snipped off two pieces of the boy's tunic. One piece included a length of stitching.

Armas stared as she placed each cutting into its own individual evidence baggie.

"Now for the DNA sample." Dr. Stern held a cotton swab and touched the boy's forearm with it. "See? Soft."

Armas giggled.

"He really likes your evidence bags. Could he play with one?" Charlie asked. She settled her hands around the boys hips to hold him steady and keep him from hiding under the table again. "That might be a good distraction."

"Excellent idea." Dr. Stern put several cotton swabs into a large evidence bag and handed them to Armas. "For you."

He smiled and clutched the bag in a fist, while tapping the ends of the cotton swabs that stuck out of the bag.

"Can you open your mouth for me?" Dr. Stern asked.

The boy shook his head and squished his lips together.

Charlie plucked one of the swabs out of the baggie and touched him playfully on the cheeks. *"Un, due, tre."* She tapped him once on the nose, once on the ear, and once on his lips.

Armas laughed.

Dr. Stern quickly inserted the swab in his mouth and swept along the inner cheek.

Armas bit down on the swab with a grunt.

"Armas!" scolded Charlie "Open your mouth."

He shook his head.

Dr. Stern smiled. "It's okay, Charlie. But too bad, because I had something for Armas." She stuck her hand in her coat pocket and pulled out a wrapped butterscotch candy.

Charlie grinned at her cleverness. *"Caramella,"* she explained.

The boy's frown melted away. *"Cos'è?"* he mumbled with the swab sticking out of his mouth.

Dr. Stern took the opportunity to pull out the swab, stick it in an evidence bag, and hold out the candy to him. "Here."

He touched the plastic wrapper. *"Cos'è?"*

"Caramella." Charlie took the candy and unwrapped it so Armas could watch. *"Lo mangi."*

Without hesitation, the boy opened his mouth. Charlie popped the candy into it, and a wide smile broke out on his face.

"Caramella," he said. *"Adoro le caramelle."*

What little boy didn't love candy?

"Do you think you retrieved a good enough sample?" Commander Orr stood next to Stormy.

Dr. Stern placed the sample baggies in her case and snapped it shut. "I think so. I'll send these to the lab at NSA in the morning."

Commander Orr observed the boy as he sucked on his butterscotch. "Please ask them to do a compare to the sample we collected at Devils Lake."

"Do you think the boy could be connected?" Dr. Stern stood and joined Orr in the office beyond the darkened conference room.

"At this point, I don't know what to believe, but it's all I've got."
He yawned. "Maybe there will be a connection, or maybe I'm crazy."

"True. I'll let the lab know." Dr. Stern took a glance at Charlie
and Armas. "Where will you take him this late?"

"Until we have those results, he should be kept out of sight," Orr
said. "I'm not risking exposure by contacting Child Protective
Services. He should be with one of us."

Stormy stepped forward. "I'll take him."

Charlie's heart pounded. Why did the idea of giving up Armas
to someone else bother her so?

The married petty officer smiled at the boy. "He should be in a
family home. I have clothes for him. Owen's a couple of years older
than he is, and his old stuff should fit him."

"Excellent, Petty Officer Storm." Orr nodded. "I know it's a little
unusual, but your main job, until we know more about those test
results, will be to keep an eye on him. Stay indoors. No visitors until
we have a better grasp on this."

"Will do, sir."

Charlie hugged the little boy to her chest. "If you need help,
please let me know." Why did it feel as if she were giving up her own
child?

"Of course I will." Stormy approached the boy and knelt in front
of him, a warm smile on her face. "I'll take care of him as if he were
mine."

CHAPTER 4

CHARLIE SAT AT HER DESK. Why did she feel so bereft? Stormy had carried Armas away, and now her arms were empty. Although she knew Stormy would do right by the orphaned child, she couldn't shake the strange feeling that washed over her when she handed him off.

Odd how close she felt to a boy she'd only met a few hours ago.

Only she, Demarco, and Orr remained in the office. The clock on the wall quietly ticked the moments away. To go back to her motel room and try to sleep seemed impossible. Her mind worked a million miles a minute.

"Tired?" Special Agent Demarco asked. He stood a few feet distant in his usual rigid pose.

Commander Orr had holed up in his office talking with someone on the phone, his back turned.

"Not anymore." She turned on her computer screen and navigated to her protected folder with her Voynich translations.

"You aren't seriously going to work on that now, right?" He crossed his arms.

"If it bothers you, no, I'm not working on it." She clicked open the PDF of the manuscript and searched for the pages she remembered.

"Yes, you are." He snorted what sounded like a laugh. "I'm standing right here. I can see you."

Demarco was so annoying. "Why do you care?" Why didn't he just go home and leave her to her work?

He casually closed in on her cubical. "Touchy, touchy."

She paused and faced him. "Aren't you the least bit curious about Armas? The pod? What exactly is going on?"

"Of course I am." His defensive wall cracked open a few centimeters, and his shoulders relaxed.

"Then why aren't you asking questions? Why aren't you digging for more information?" She couldn't stop the emotions from flowing freely and concluded with her true issue. "Why did you let Chief jump down my throat out there when you knew my story was the truth?"

He paused before answering. "I need more evidence."

Right. Of course. Even though she'd swam back to shore with the boy in her arms, he needed even more evidence. His own eyes weren't good enough. Good God, he was infuriating.

"Evidence of what? Armas is no alien. He's a human boy who speaks Italian and English. Let's just start there. And remember, the manuscript has connections to Rome."

"I thought you said in your presentation the origins were unknown." He cocked his head.

"Voynich claimed the manuscript had its origins in southern Europe, and last time I checked Italy would be considered southern Europe."

Demarco's brow knit together. "Just spit it out already."

"Spit what out?"

"Clearly, you want me to come to some conclusion. You claim to wonder about the boy, then prod me for answers to questions you already have answered in your own head. Sorry, but I'm not that good at mind reading, Cutter."

Charlie bit her tongue. Why was he being such a...such a...ugh.

Why did he have to be right? "Fine. I'll tell you what I think is in the manuscript that might connect to Armas and what's really going on here."

"Finally."

She narrowed her eyes then turned back to her computer screen. "Remember yesterday I told you that someone in the ancient past was building pods? Machines out of organic materials?"

She scrolled past the page where she'd partially translated the symbols that led her to that conclusion. "Well, there's more. And after what happened tonight, I think we need to reanalyze the purpose of this office and our team."

"Go on." Commander Orr joined them.

Charlie's heart sped up and her palms grew sweaty. She'd set up a meeting with Orr for Monday morning, but now it seemed as if she might as well go for it. Either they'd think she was crazy, or maybe they'd see what she did in the ancient text.

"I'd started translating this section, but it didn't make a whole lot of sense until tonight." She'd scrolled to a page that had the chronological year drawn in a circle. "These notes here." She pointed to a corner of the page.

"What does it say?" Orr asked quietly.

Did he already know what she was going to tell them?

"'Calculate arrival year.'" She hadn't translated everything on the page. She pointed to another clump of text. "And here, 'five hundred years in total.'"

Both men stood silently.

The next bit might freak them out.

"And then here, next to this picture of a pod." She pointed to a small drawing on the opposite page with script underneath. "He is not safe here."

Demarco's face turned ashen. He took a step back.

Orr took a quick glance at his head of security. "Well, Petty Officer? Fill in the gaps please."

"The pod wasn't an alien spacecraft. It never was." Charlie took a deep breath to calm herself before she spoke. Would these men think her insane? "The pod is a time machine. Armas traveled through time."

Orr stroked his jaw and had a blank stare. "How is that even possible?"

Demarco paced the aisle between the cubicles. Each exhale escaped his nose in a loud gust of air as if he were a bull waiting on the bullfighter's approach in the ring.

What kept Charlie sane and able to speak was the text in front of her. Focusing on the translations and the written word grounded her in something real. Something believable. Even when it was completely unbelievable. "It's a lot to grasp. I know. But Armas is living proof these translations are correct. Everything about him convinces me he came from the fifteenth century."

The door opened and Kellerman entered. "Sorry about that. I had a little bit of a delay." He scanned the room for a moment. "Hey, where'd everybody go?"

"It's only the three of us," Charlie said. Demarco's silence weighed on her. What did he think about her statement? For some reason, she really wanted his support of her theory. His buy-in would mean he trusted her, he believed her.

Kellerman frowned.

"Lieutenant," Orr said. "We need you caught up with the latest information. I want to hear your input on Petty Officer Cutter's theory. Please, join us."

Maybe she'd made a mistake announcing her idea to the two men. She'd been burned in the past with her declarations and even became so frustrated with her work, she'd quit it altogether. In her head, she knew she was right. But she'd needed the validation of the text to support her idea. The minute Armas had exited the pod, she knew this boy was not of the modern world, and surely wasn't an alien. When he'd leapt into her arms a connection was made. A connection unlike any other she'd ever experienced. It was as if she knew Armas on some deep level. A déjà vu. Something about him had been familiar and unfamiliar all at the same time. And if she had confessed such things on the shore of the Occoquan River, her whole team would have thought her crazy.

She stared across the aisle at Demarco. He wouldn't meet her gaze. Why?

"A theory?" Kellerman approached the small group. "Did Dr. Stern gather her samples already?"

"Yes, she's going to have them compare the boy's DNA sample to the earlier pod samples," the commander said. "Dr. Stern told me the clothing can be analyzed immediately. A report should be available Monday. Petty Officer Storm took charge of the boy. Until we know more, he'll remain in her care."

Kellerman nodded. "So what's this about a theory?" He shifted his gaze to Charlie.

Why did she wish she could present her work in the conference room to the entire team, rather than late at night to only a few? Some rest and a bit of perspective might be warranted before delving too deeply into the topic.

She swallowed. "I was just explaining that after Armas's arrival, I thought again about some of the translations I'd worked on yesterday, and how I think we have this all wrong. These aren't alien pods. These are ancient time machines we've been chasing—from the time period when the manuscript was written."

Kellerman laughed. "What?"

Out of all of the people on the team, she didn't expect that from serious, nerdy Kellerman. Why did his response bother her so much? Worse than when Chief accused her of lying about Armas.

"Hey, give her some respect, Cole." Demarco broke his silence and stepped forward.

Charlie locked eyes with Demarco, and a shiver ran through her.

Without looking away, he continued, "What I witnessed tonight makes no sense. At least Cutter has an explanation for it. I still want results from Dr. Stern's tests, but at the very least, we must accept all theories this team produces until evidence proves one of them wrong."

Thank you, Charlie mouthed.

Demarco answered with a small nod.

"A time machine. That's literally impossible." Kellerman took a wide stance and crossed his arms. "I'm supposed to believe someone in the fifteenth century figured something out that nobody in the twenty-first century has even come close to creating?"

"For now, yes," Orr said. "I'll admit the possibility has my mind reeling. I have to reset my thinking and build up a new plan." He snapped his fingers. "Kellerman, I told Chief he'd be working with you tomorrow on the radar signature data. Wouldn't that give us some information about whether or not this new theory has any legs?"

Kellerman had visible tension in his neck and shoulders. He rubbed his brow. "It might."

"An alien craft should have a full trajectory that we can plot through the atmosphere. I'd like to know if we have a complete signature or a partial signature. When and where did these pods appear on our radar?"

"Right." Kellerman avoided eye contact with Charlie. "Chief and I can do that."

"Tomorrow at 0800," the commander said. "I wish I could ask more about your translation work, Cutter. But I know it's late, and we all need some sort of rest before tomorrow. Is this what you wanted to talk to me about on Monday?"

"Yes, sir. I know you wanted me to translate the pod writings first, but—"

He waved a hand. "We're past that now. Clearly, you have proven to me the manuscript has more clues for us to follow. A time machine—" He covered his mouth with his hand. "Unbelievable."

"Can we go, sir?" asked Kellerman.

"Yes, please. We'll all be back in the morning to discuss further. Stormy will stay home with the boy. Now he has much more significance than I originally thought." Commander Orr eyes glowed. "Truly something miraculous."

As the team prepared to leave, Demarco remained by Charlie's desk.

She picked up her purse and slipped on her dark navy cardigan over her sleeveless top. Why was he hovering there?

"I'd like to walk you to your room." He erased the distance between them.

Kellerman and Orr had already left the office.

Her heart fluttered in her chest. "That's not necessary."

"I need to talk to you."

He touched her arm, and it seared like a hot coal against her skin.

———

Demarco and Cutter strolled side by side toward the base motel under the glaring street lights. The Washington Navy Yard was devoid of life with the exception of two cars, which drove toward the barracks at a crawl.

How different her life would've been if she'd kept her original orders after graduating from DLI. She thought fleetingly of her roommate, a quiet girl from North Carolina who'd been a Persian-Farsi linguist. She'd probably be graduating soon and headed to Bahrain.

The cars parked and several sailors emptied out. All young men. All drunk. They stumbled along singing a Lady Gaga song and laughing at each other.

A different life entirely.

"Idiots." Demarco had noticed them, too. "Life is short, and that's how they want to spend it?"

"What are you? A hundred years old?" She continued to watch the drunk men. If only she had friends who would laugh with her the same way. "They're only having some fun."

"There's more important things to do." He turned away from the revelry.

She sighed. Of course, boring Demarco only wanted to hang out with his plants and impress Dr. Stern. Anything else was a waste of time. "So, what did you want to talk to me about?"

He slowed his pace. "About your theory."

She glanced around. "Out here?"

"Nobody can hear us." He gestured at the empty streets.

"So it's okay to break the rules when Demarco says it's okay. Got it." Could he hear the sarcasm in her voice?

"Angel. When we're not in the office, I'd like you to call me that."

Her breath quickened. "What? Why?"

He stopped by a bench for the base bus and gestured at her to take a seat. "Do you mind?"

The hard crusty exterior she'd always imagined surrounded Demarco—no, Angel—had vanished. "I guess not." She sat at the very end of the bench leaving plenty of room.

Angel sat so close to her their thighs touched.

She moved one inch to the left. His presence overwhelmed her in a very confusing way. Her mind whizzed through all of the Demarcos she'd encountered in her first week at her new job: angry, kind, distant, polite, annoyed, and now—?

"I want to be able to trust you, Charlie." He turned slightly so their eyes met.

"We all need to trust each other on the team." She shifted uncomfortably in her seat as his dark eyes softened.

He shook his head. "That's not what I mean. I haven't been able to find anyone I felt I could confide in for a long time."

Her breathing grew shallow, and her ears rang. What did he

mean? "Clarissa, your date, she seemed nice." Beautiful slinky Clarissa in the blue dress. He so clearly preferred that kind of woman over someone like her. "I'm nobody. I'm nothing."

"You're not nothing."

"What could you possibly need to tell me that you couldn't tell Stormy or the commander or Kellerman?"

"Kellerman?" He snorted. "I'd never confide in that pompous ass."

Charlie's mind raced. What was happening here? "My theory. You wanted to discuss it. Well?"

"Right." He leaned back and faced the street, breaking the intense eye contact. "After what we experienced tonight, I think we both know your theory is the correct one."

Well, that was an unexpected admission from the dour and doubtful Angel Demarco. He thought her idea had merit?

"I thought you wanted to wait for Dr. Stern to do her tests?" she asked. "You made that very clear to Chief Ricard anyway."

"I'm sorry about that, Charlie," he said. "I was still in shock. But when I took a closer look at the boy, saw his reactions, and then the translations...well, I'm convinced. I know what Dr. Stern's tests are going to say."

"You believe me?" She studied the pleasing outline of his face in the harsh glare of the bright streetlights.

"Yes."

"You don't think it's crazy or that I'm being silly?"

"No."

Her mouth gaped at his answer. "I don't even know what to say."

"Can I ask you more about the manuscript?" He faced her. "What else have you translated? Any other clues about the machine, the boy, anything at all?"

The directness of his gaze made her glance away. "Well, it's a pretty large manuscript, and I've only begun to create the translitera-tions and do the comparisons."

He cupped her chin and gently tipped up her face. "I'm interested. I'd really like to know, Charlie."

Their faces were inches apart. A slight breeze blew her hair across her eyes. He swept away the strands and leaned in.

Was he going to kiss her?

CHAPTER 5

NOBODY else besides maybe her advisor in grad school had ever shown much interest in the manuscript translation. And, here, in front of her was an attractive, interested man who truly appeared to want to know more.

Whose mouth hovered above hers.

How could she resist?

"I wish tonight I could've spent more time explaining—" God, could she not stop talking? As weird as it seemed, an odd thrill ran through her at the thought of Angel Demarco kissing her on a bus bench.

"Shh—"

His mouth descended on hers, taking the very breath from her.

So unexpected, so surprising, and so...wow...thrilling.

He pulled her closer and their bodies met. His hard chest against hers. She knew the solid muscle that existed beneath the dress shirt, and her hands were eager to touch. Instead, she curled her hands around his waist.

She wanted to pause time and stay in the moment forever.

How was it possible the man had such soft lips? Everything about him was hard: his clipped speech, his stare, his judgment, his body.

The kiss deepened and became more wild, more uncontrolled.

Why did they have to kiss out here? In the open?

They should be in a private place, in the dark, where they could explore everything. Where she could shift his hands from caressing her jaw to removing her clothes.

Without reason or warning, Angel ended it.

He pushed gently on her shoulders. "I shouldn't have done that." He breathed heavily.

She nodded absentmindedly. "Right." Her lips burned. She wanted more. She didn't want him to stop, which made her mind spin in circles.

His cheeks were flushed, and his pupils were dilated. "Definitely not," he whispered.

"What would Clarissa think?" she blurted out. Why was she unable to shut off the rush of heat to her center? He said he'd made a mistake. He was right. She hated him...well, hate was a strong word...she found him irritating and cold and...dammit so ridiculously sexy.

He stroked a thumb down her cheek. "We can't do this."

"Angel—"

Her saying his name seemed to hit him like a physical blow.

Letting out a grunt, he stood. "I can't do this. Everything about it is wrong." He stroked his jaw. "Shit. Shit. Shit."

He paced along the edge of the sidewalk.

"It was only a kiss." She clamped down on her body's responses. Willed them away. It had been too long since a man had touched her like that. She was starved for affection, that had to be it. It wasn't Angel she was attracted to, but the idea of anyone being attracted to her.

"I'll never do that again. I apologize Petty Officer Cutter." He kept his gaze angled away.

"Okay." How could she hide the disappointment in her voice? He'd unlocked feelings inside her she didn't know she had.

He kicked the bus stop pole full force. "Fuck."

Charlie shrunk back. "Let's forget it ever happened."

He met her gaze. "I never expected this...you don't understand." His posture stiffened and muscles grew rigid.

"The best thing to do then is drop it." Everything in her screamed 'no,' but his reaction had been so desperate and angry, what else could she do? "I'll never bring it up again."

Her throat choked up. Why was this so hard for her?

He nodded. His warm brown eyes cooled within seconds.

"You wanted to ask me more about the manuscript?" She shivered in the cooling air. Earlier tonight he'd offered her his shirt, but chivalry like that probably would end.

"Yes." He made no move to join her on the bench again.

"Then ask away." The excitement that had taken flight when the special agent showed interest in her discoveries had just had its wings clipped.

———

Angel Demarco remained standing a distance away from Charlie and cleared this throat. "Explain it to me. The translations you're working on."

She lifted her chin to meet his gaze. Although her stomach hardened after his rejection, she wasn't about to let him think he'd hurt her. He was a jerk. A player. A heartbreaker. She'd narrowly avoided being another of his conquests.

"I noticed right away an emphasis on time in the manuscript drawings. The celestial calendar." Better to focus on her work. Facts over feelings. If he was interested in the manuscript, at least they could have that in common. "The depiction of the cycles of the moon, the movement of the constellations across the sky, the shift of the Earth throughout the seasons. Not every page, but many of them."

He broke eye contact.

As she spoke, she was able to tamp down her hurt. Translation work was her passion. Her life. It could fill any hole she had...especially one created by Demarco. "That led me to wonder why. Why so much about the passage of time and seasons? And then when I crafted the transliteration alphabet and decoded what I could, I knew these pods had been built using some kind of formula. An organic machine made without electronics, at least electronics we'd recognize in the modern era. Bioelectric, perhaps? The science part of it isn't my area. We'd need the help of Kellerman to maybe make sense of it."

He paced in front of her. "And you knew humans created these pods?"

"Not right away. No. When I arrived, I was told we were hunting aliens, so, of course, I assumed this was built off of proof, evidence, factual information that I had yet to see for myself. I trusted the team."

He nodded. The rigidity she'd grown used to seeing in his posture had returned.

Why couldn't she stop thinking about the lightness of his touch on her cheek? The feel of his body against hers?

Dammit. Focus, Charlie. Focus. He doesn't want you.

"When Armas came out of the pod, that's when I knew." Her heart softened at the memory. Poor little thing. "That's when I understood that everything I'd been told about the pods had been wrong. The Voynich manuscript was written by a human hand over five hundred years ago. These time machines were built by human beings. There are no aliens."

He bit his lip. "Is there a name in the manuscript? Any indication of who wrote it?"

Interesting questions he had.

"I don't know. There are dozens of pages to translate. I focused on the ones that had the most relatable phonemes to the writing found in the pods, and those were all related to movement and flight. But now that we have Armas...and we know for sure we are dealing with a human in the past who wrote this text, I hope I can find more. Someone built a pod for Armas. For some reason he was in danger."

"Yes. True." His voice trailed off, and he rubbed his forehead. "I wonder why?"

"I don't know, but if I was his mother, I wouldn't want to send him into a future alone." How could any mother who loved her child send him in a pod into the unknown? Her mind shifted to the one that had exploded in Idaho. If that had been Armas? A pain hit the back of her throat.

"His mother—" He covered his mouth and turned away from her.

"I suppose it could be his father who put him in the pod." The focus on the manuscript helped improve her mindset, center herself on her work. "But since he asked for his mother the whole time, I guess I made an assumption."

"Right. That makes sense." He paused in his pacing and stared into the distance. "Should we keep walking?"

Yes, the whole purpose was to walk her safely back to her room. Whatever his original intent had been, the electricity between them earlier had faded.

She stood and wrapped her arms around her body. The air had cooled, and the humidity made everything damp. They walked side by side with two feet of space between them.

"But it might help if I can translate more of the text, so I can figure out exactly why Armas was the only person in the pod," Charlie said.

"We've never encountered a pod with more than one occupant."

"I thought we'd never reached a pod soon enough to know how many occupants were inside." She stopped in her tracks. How had she forgotten? "Oh my God. I've been so focused on Armas, I didn't think about the other pods. Last summer one landed. Then the one in Idaho, which exploded." The thought of it made her shiver.

"And then the one at Devils Lake in North Dakota."

"You never did tell me what happened in the woods after Kellerman and the chief were attacked."

"Nothing happened." He threw up his hands "I thought I saw a figure far ahead in the trees. But it turned out to be nothing."

"Someone hit the chief."

"True."

"We need to go back." With this new knowledge, how could they do anything less?

"To North Dakota?"

"Yes, now that we know these are human beings. Time travelers. Can you even imagine someone dealing with a modern world?" As she thought more deeply about it, her steps slowed. "It would be a huge shock. For a child, maybe easier. It's been a week. Maybe there's been an encounter. Eventually, this traveler will need food, water, shelter."

"We can bring it up to the commander tomorrow. See what he thinks."

"I want Armas to have his parents with him." How sad for the boy to have no one. Not a parent, not a relative, not a friend. Only A Group. They were his family now. "I want him to feel safe again. I want him to have someone in this world who cares about him."

"You care about him," Demarco said softly.

Why did he have to be so kind? It would be easier to deny her attraction if he would be cold and distant Demarco. "He's only a little boy. Anyone would feel the way I do."

"Would they?" He drew closer to her. "I know you feel responsible for him. That's understandable. You rescued him from drowning alone in the river."

She shuddered. "The poor little thing."

"If the pod in North Dakota connects to Armas, we need to know."

He had closed the gap between them, so much so she could feel the heat of his body. How was she going to work with him, if she couldn't rid herself of these stupid feelings?

She took a breath, and steadied her mind. They were work colleagues only. The kiss had been a mistake. "What if that person is the author of the manuscript? I have so many questions."

"We all do."

They reached her temporary living quarters.

"Guess this is where I say 'Good night.'" His dark eyes glittered in the exterior lights near the motel entrance.

A rush of nervous energy filled her. "You could come up?" Why did she want to make a fool of herself?

His skin flushed, and his hands clenched briefly. He opened his mouth to speak. "Yes." Angel Demarco's demeanor shifted almost imperceptibly.

But Charlie recognized it. She'd been paired up with this man in enough situations that she could see it. The softening around the mouth. The relaxation of his shoulders. The hesitant step toward her.

Had she misjudged him?

"Yes?" she whispered. Mostly to herself because she still couldn't believe she asked him to come up to her room after his flat out rejection. She expected a derisive laugh. A cutting remark. Who was this man? How could the most difficult person she'd ever encountered intrigue her so much?

He guided her by the elbow through the main entrance. "You've seen my apartment, I think I deserve to see yours."

The heat of his hand through the thin cardigan was welcome. But was this merely a friendly visit? Or something more? "I see. Turnabout is fair play?" Easier to make a joke than confront the strong feelings she had for him.

The night clerk watched from his position behind the front desk as they crossed through the lobby. He glanced from Charlie to

Angel, read the situation, and returned to the paperback book he had in his hands.

Charlie's heart pounded.

They navigated to the bank of elevators in silence.

Demarco pressed the 'up' button. "We aren't enemies, Charlie."

The low rumble of his voice caused goose bumps to rise on her flesh. What was this game he was playing with her?

She said nothing.

The display above them showed an elevator descending from the third floor.

In a few moments, the door of Elevator 1 opened, and he helped her inside. The doors closed with a whoosh.

Standing in the quiet compartment away from any prying eyes made her bolder in her words. "I don't understand you." She shook off his grasp. "One minute you're annoyed with me, the next you're kissing me. What did I do to make you treat me that way?" Clarissa had been his date for the evening. That was the type she'd assumed he'd go for. Gorgeous. Perfect in every way. Feminine. "Am I not good enough for you? Pretty enough? Smart enough?"

He pressed his hand against her stomach and forced her back to the wall. His gaze burned into her. "You're all of those things and more, Charlie."

Warmth rushed to her center.

His mouth hovered over hers. Breath light on her face. "Why can't I get you out of my head?"

Her mouth parted. "I don't know."

His kiss was harder the second time. Needier.

She looped her arms around his neck and drew him to her. Closer. Closer. Closer.

Their bodies pressed together as if melded together by heat alone.

Charlie drew in his scent, fresh yet masculine. Green like the jungle of plants in his apartment. Who was this strange man who'd despised her on day one? Criticized her?

She didn't care.

He kissed down her neck and mumbled her name.

The elevator dinged.

They broke apart and stared for a moment at the open door. Her floor. Her room. Only twenty feet away.

Angel threw out an arm to block the door from closing. "What do you want to do?"

They stood in a tight embrace.

Charlie didn't want to let go.

He stared down at her. Fire in his eyes.

Her hands slid up his neck and cupped his jaw. "This is what I want to do." She kissed him slowly, gently.

When she finished the kiss, their foreheads touched. Angel breathed heavily.

The door attempted to close.

"God help me." He grunted, scooped her up in solid arms, and carried her into the hall. "Which room is yours?"

CHAPTER 6

THE VIBRATION of her phone on the nightstand woke her. A text had come in.

She stretched, and her bare leg touched the warm body of Angel Demarco. Naked. In her bed. And she wasn't regretful.

She rolled over, taking the sheet with her, and read the text from her brother, Chad:

> Family dinner. Tonight at mom and dad's. Six o'clock?

"Anyone ever tell you that you're a bed hog?"

The deep rumble of Angel Demarco's morning voice caused a flush across her body. "No." She smiled to herself. "It's cold in here. You want me to freeze?"

His arm curled across her middle, and he pulled her to him. "I'll keep you warm."

She shivered and set the phone down. "It's seven o'clock." It would be nearly impossible to think straight at the office after last night, but what choice did she have? "We have an hour to get to work."

"Do you think he'd notice if we showed up late?" He trailed light kisses down her exposed shoulder.

Her breath hitched in her throat.

How were they going to hide this from their co-workers? Damn. "I wish we had time to talk about last night—" Was it a one-time thing? Did he have feelings for her beyond a night in bed? "But we have a lot to discuss today. I want to know how Armas is doing. And if the commander is open to our idea of going back to North Dakota."

Demarco rolled onto his back. "All business with you, huh?" He let out a heavy sigh. "Got it. Back to work. Let's do this."

She reached for him as he climbed out of bed. "I didn't mean work is more important than what happened." A tingling swept up the back of her neck and across her face. Everything about last night was incredible, unexpected, and supremely satisfying. Did he think they were going to go back to normal after that?

"Is it all right if I take a shower?" He stood naked and perfect in front of her.

She swallowed. "Yes. Absolutely." Her gaze jumped to his face.

He offered a bemused smile. "Glad to know I made an impression."

"We need to talk."

He crossed the room to the bathroom. "Talk. Is that what you call it?"

As he closed the door behind him, she could hear him chuckle.

Once he turned on the shower, she picked up her phone. Staring at the request from her brother, a lump formed in her throat. Everything inside her said to beg off a family dinner. A very attractive, very interesting man was in her shower. She'd rather explore that further after work rather than defend her life choices at the dinner table. But she found herself texting back:

> Can you pick me up at five? I need a ride.

Would Chad be able to read her when he walked in the door?

Probably. Even though most of the world believed it was only identical twins who had a special connection, she and Chad had considered their twin-ness as unique. The day Charlie had decided to drop out of her master's program, Chad had called her. Out of the blue. They hadn't spoken in weeks. In fact, they hadn't spoken since Christmas when he'd gifted her with a word origin dictionary. Only Chad seemed to understand her obsession with languages and words.

Until Demarco.

Her pulse quickened.

Her phone pinged.

Yes. See you at five.

Yeah, Chad would know. She might as well start practicing her story right now. How they met. Why this guy. Could Chad meet him. All the awful stuff that was way too early to think about, but totally necessary because it was her brother.

"Don't you have any normal soap?" Angel's muffled voice interrupted her thoughts.

"Normal?"

"Like a bar of soap. You know, soap?"

"The body gel. That's soap."

"That's not soap."

"Yes, it is. Just put it on the pouf and—" She giggled. Would burly, manly Angel actually pour lavender body gel onto a bright pink puff?

"Forget it. I'm just going to use the shampoo."

"Hurry up." Charlie checked the time on her phone. Seven fifteen. Shit. "We can't show up at the same time."

"Why not?"

The shower shut off.

"Then everyone will know." Why did she have to explain this to him? Was he that incapable of thinking about the implications at the office?

The bathroom door opened. "So?"

She gulped. He'd wrapped a towel around his waist. Somehow that made him even more attractive than when he had been one-hundred percent naked only a few minutes earlier. "Well, wouldn't that be wrong or illegal or something?"

"It's not illegal to date someone in the office."

They were dating? Okay. Not a one-night thing. Good. Or bad? What if Stormy had been right about Angel? "Right."

"Your turn." He nodded at the open bathroom door, and his eyes lit up. "I can help if you want."

"I think I've got it." How in the world was she going to handle this? She had important, life-changing work to do. She had to find a way to keep her love life from interfering with possibly the most amazing discovery in history.

First work. Then dinner with her messed up family. Then maybe time to ponder the implications of having sex with Angel Demarco.

———

Impossible though it seemed, Angel and Charlie had arrived at the office together at five minutes before eight o'clock and nobody batted an eye. He'd headed straight for the coffee at the back of the room, and she'd taken up where she'd left off with her translation work.

Although for the first five or ten minutes, she'd had a difficult time shaking off memories of last night, the familiar loops and whorls of the Voynich text soon took over. The translations were coming faster now, which seemed impossible. Scholars spent their whole careers on this text and had come up with nothing. She'd discovered a few clues from a pod, and now she was whisking through the pages and uncovering the true meaning of the manuscript. An impossibility in graduate school, yet here she was succeeding with the support of her team.

And yet she wouldn't be able to share that success with her family tonight. Although they knew she'd been brought on for her linguistics background and that she'd requested her Voynich work, that's as far as she could take it. Her work was classified, and so was her accomplishment. If only she could explain to her father, maybe he'd finally be proud of her, like her brother Chad.

Why did she have to care so much about what her father thought of her and her career? Inside, she burned with the desire to bring him into the fold and tell him everything about what they discovered. The pods. The translations. Armas. The ancient time machine. All of it. Oh, what a fantastic conversation they could have. Two adults working in the world of classified material. What had he seen and experienced all of those years in the NSA? She'd never asked, but now she understood better the burden he must carry.

"So while I wait for Chief to show up, walk me through these translations of yours." Kellerman stood a few feet from her cubicle. "Chief didn't seem so keen on your story about Armas, and if you catch me up on what you've uncovered, maybe I can advocate for you. He's pretty stubborn, if you haven't figured it out already."

"Stubborn?" Charlie spun in her chair to face the lieutenant. "He was rude and condescending. He accused me of being a liar."

Kellerman tucked his hands under his armpits and leaned against the cubicle wall opposite her. "It's all about rank to him. He's an E-7, you're an E-4. You made him look bad in front of Commander Orr."

She let out a laugh. "How did I make him look bad?" The egos of some of the military men she'd encountered were ridiculous.

"Chief's been on this team since the beginning, and he has yet to encounter a pod landing right in front of his eyes—"

"It had already landed."

"Or being the first on the scene."

"I just happened to be in the vicinity." She shrugged. "He should be made of tougher stuff than that."

"You don't want to be on Chief's bad side," Kellerman warned. "He's a good guy, if you give him a chance."

"I did nothing to deserve being on his 'bad side.'"

The door opened and Chief Ricard walked in. "Good morning, everyone."

Charlie turned back to her computer screen. "Maybe you should move along and do that radar work the commander wanted the two of you to focus on."

"Is there a problem here?" Demarco strolled down the aisle, a mug of coffee in each hand.

Oh, God, not now Angel. Not now.

"No, no problem," Kellerman said straightening up.

"Good." The special agent set a mug of coffee right next to Charlie's keyboard. "Thought you could use an extra cup this morning."

Shit.

Kellerman raised a brow, noting the gesture. "Hey, weren't you wearing that shirt last night?" he asked Demarco.

Why didn't Angel stop at his Landcruiser and swap shirts with one in his go-bag, like she'd suggested on their walk to work?

Angel looked down at his shirt and then glanced at Charlie. "I like this shirt. Something wrong with wearing it two days in a row?" He winked at her when Kellerman wasn't looking.

Lieutenant Kellerman said nothing for a couple of beats.

Charlie could feel his stare weighing her down, judging her. He knew. He absolutely knew. And he'd asked her out only a couple of days ago. Her stomach roiled. Why did she put herself in this position? She should've left Angel standing outside her motel room last night. This mess was all of her own doing.

"LT," said Chief in a booming voice that was far too loud for eight o'clock on a Sunday morning. "Let's get cracking on the data."

"There's a rank system here, Petty Officer, even if you don't like it," Kellerman said. "No matter what someone else might tell you." He stared daggers at Demarco as he joined the chief on the other side of the small office.

Angel stepped closer to her cubicle. "What's his problem?"

Charlie sipped on the hot coffee he'd brought her. "Did you really have to do that?"

"Do what?"

"You know."

"Why don't you explain it to me tonight at dinner?" His eyes shone.

The same low rumble he'd spoken with that morning returned melting her insides.

"I can't."

He lifted his chin, and his body stiffened into the Demarco she'd known before last night. "Oh?"

"Team," Commander Orr announced from the entrance to his office. "Looks like we're all here. Let's meet in the conference room and discuss next steps and bring the chief up to speed on last night's discovery, shall we?"

Angel frowned.

"Let's talk later?" she offered.

"Sure," he said coolly and headed toward the conference room.

———

Commander Orr stood behind the podium. "Before we launch into last night, I heard from Petty Officer Storm a little while ago."

Charlie leaned forward in her seat.

Demarco sat to her left with his arms crossed.

"Armas is doing well. Despite the strange circumstances of his arrival, he's eating, he slept well, and he's playing with her two children."

"Did you call CPS?" Chief asked.

"No, Chief," Orr said. "We decided until we hear back from Dr. Stern, we should keep the boy under wraps."

Ricard snorted, but said nothing more. He knew when he was outranked. Orr had the say for how Armas would be treated.

"Next, I wanted to let all of you know Kellerman will be heading out on special assignment later today."

Charlie stared across the conference table at the lieutenant. What was this all about?

Orr held up his hands. "I know this comes out of left field, as we are supposed to act as a team. But last night's discovery, Petty Officer Cutter's translation work, and other information has led me to believe we need to go back to North Dakota."

Could it be possible Orr came to the same conclusion as she? That if Armas came from the past, then the other pod most likely held another human from the past? Maybe Armas's mother?

"Sir," Demarco said. "Why Kellerman? He has no training in tracking or investigations of this sort." His brow furrowed.

"Last night, Kellerman met with a contact."

Charlie thought back to last night when Kellerman arrived later to the office than everyone else, and Orr had mentioned he'd maybe stopped for gas or something. "Who?"

"I'll let Kellerman share that with you." The commander gestured at him. "Lieutenant?"

The young officer stood, straightening his khaki uniform pants. Typically, he wore civilian clothes, so it was notable he'd chosen to wear his uniform on a Sunday trip to the office. "Thank you, sir."

Negative vibes rolled off of Demarco, as if his skin were covered with visible prickles.

How easily she could read him now. Has she been able to do that before they'd had sex? Or was this a new ability she'd acquired?

"This is a huge mistake," the special agent said.

"Angel." Charlie touched his arm and instantly regretted it.

Chief's eyes narrowed, and his gaze shifted from Demarco to Charlie and back again.

"Agent Demarco," the commander said with clipped speech. "You will give the lieutenant some respect. Back off." The older man stood to the side of the podium to let Kellerman approach.

In his uniform khakis the lieutenant appeared older and more mature. He braced his hands on either side of the podium and connected his gaze with each person in the room. "We weren't the only agency tracking the pod last night. As everyone knows, I transferred here from an assignment at the Nevada Test and Training Range in Nevada at Groom Lake or Area 51." Kellerman used air quotes when he spoke the well-known nickname. "Although I cannot divulge the work I participated in at that facility, I still have contacts there. The radar signature data was collected through the NGA, or National Geospatial-Intelligence Agency, and that data is shared throughout the Department of Defense."

"What does any of this have to do with you needing to go to North Dakota by yourself?" Demarco spat out.

"Patience, Special Agent." Orr gave him a pointed look.

"My contact also tracked the landing in Devils Lake for their own purposes. They've run into a situation that needs my assistance."

"Situation?" Charlie asked. Did someone find a passenger from the earlier pod?

"They've recovered a body from the area near the landing site. My contact was aware of our office and thought we should have access to samples."

Why did she feel so nauseated all of a sudden? A body? In what condition?

"Why did this contact believe the body was connected to the pod?" Demarco asked.

"It wasn't until I came back to the office and heard about Cutter's translation work that I realized how important that body could be," explained Kellerman. "It was found maybe a hundred yards from where the chief and I were attacked. And one other unusual thing." Kellerman picked up the iPad he usually carried. "The body had a strange deformity."

He tapped on the screen to bring up a photo.

When he turned the iPad to show them, Charlie gasped.

Deformed feet with a single big toe and a split like a vee with another malformed toe splitting off in the other direction.

Just like the footprints she'd seen in the sand.

The footprints Demarco had convinced her didn't exist.

What was going on?

CHAPTER 7

"WHAT IN THE FUCK?" Chief declared at the sight of the photo on the iPad. "What is that?"

"A strange deformation of the feet," Kellerman said. "Genetic problem of some kind."

Demarco slumped in his seat.

Why did Angel try to convince her the footprints she'd seen hadn't been real? "I saw footprints like that on the beach, near the woods," she confessed.

"Why didn't you document this?" asked the commander.

She lifted her chin. "Special Agent Demarco told me I was seeing things." How could she do anything less than tell the truth? They all needed to know what she'd witnessed that day. Those strange feet had to have been the ones to make those footprints. "I'm quite sure the body connects to the pod. That has to be the passenger."

Angel tilted away from her.

Everything they'd shared last night in her motel room disappeared, and it was as if they were back at square one. That first day rushed back to her mind. How annoyed he'd been with her. How certain he was that she was a burden on the team and not an asset.

"Demarco, I'd like to meet with you later in my office," the commander said.

Angel barely nodded. His gaze turned inward, and it was as if he checked out completely from the team.

Any intimacy they shared faded.

"Tell me more, Petty Officer Cutter," Orr said.

"After Chief and the lieutenant arrived at the pod crash site, Special Agent Demarco had made his way down the beach. I assumed he was following tracks of some kind or some sort of evidence." Why did her insides feel as if they were on fire? She only wanted to share what she knew, so that they could figure out more about Armas, the pods, the whole mystery. But each word tore at her. She didn't want to hurt Angel, but what else could she do? He'd lied to her. "He'd left me with the pod, so I thought it was important, and I followed him. That's when I saw the tracks leading into the woods."

"This is significant. I wish we had evidence of what you saw, but since we have the body, the lieutenant will be able to retrieve it and bring it back to Dr. Stern for a thorough exam." Commander Orr stood with his feet planted solidly apart. "Kellerman, do you have any more information you'd like to share before you leave this afternoon?"

"The body found is that of a male, and he had been hit with a blunt object. Perhaps a rock or other item on the scene. They're in the middle of a storm cycle, so it will be hard to identify the murder weapon."

"Murder?" Charlie gasped.

Kellerman nodded. "Someone attacked this person. We might never know who did it or why, but at least we have the body to examine."

Dr. Stern entered the room. "A body?" She held a locked, zippered case in her hands.

"Doctor, I'm so glad you're here," Orr said. "We were about to discuss Cutter's discoveries in her translation work."

"I listened to your voicemail a little while ago. Time travel? I couldn't believe it. I want to know more." Her eyes lit up. "Since I was on my way here with my preliminary analysis of the boy's tunic, I didn't return your call." She set the case on the end of the table near the door. "But a body? Could it be another time traveler? Tell me more."

"Time travel?" Chief gawked. "Would someone like to clue me in? When did we decide on that theory?"

Orr held up a hand. "Sorry, Chief, a lot has happened since you went home last night. We'll get to that explanation in a minute."

Ricard crossed his arms, and his brows knit together. "You've got to be kidding me. You've all lost your minds. I can't wait to hear what made you all come to that conclusion."

Charlie gritted her teeth, struggling to contain her irritation at Ricard's dismissive words. First, he didn't believe Armas came out of the pod, now he pushed aside the time travel theory without even listening to her evidence.

"We'll get to that in a minute, Chief." Orr quickly summarized the discovery, "Kellerman is traveling to North Dakota today to retrieve a body that was found near the pod we investigated last week."

Dr. Stern's mouth formed an 'o.' She pulled out a chair and sat. "Incredible. You think it's related to the pod?"

Orr looked at Charlie before answering. "Yes, there seems to be a pretty solid connection between the location of the pod, the body, and some footprints discovered near the scene."

"Sounds like we're going to keep the NSA lab busy," remarked Dr. Stern. "I'm very interested in making comparisons between the blood that was recovered by Petty Officer Cutter, the body, and the boy."

How awful if the man found in North Dakota was related to

Armas. Although it would answer some questions, it would leave the boy an orphan in a strange world.

"It also appears the person in the woods had been attacked and died from his wounds," Kellerman added.

Charlie's stomach soured. Demarco had run off into the woods, leaving her to tend to an unconscious Chief and a wounded Kellerman. He'd told her later he hadn't encountered anything, but now her mind turned over the new information and doubt grew like a noxious weed. Could she trust him? He'd lied to her about the footprints and now a dead body turned up.

"Despite this astounding new discovery," began Dr. Stern. "I wanted to share with you my early analysis of the boy's clothing."

"I wasn't expecting anything so quickly, doctor," said Orr.

"I couldn't sleep much last night. All that excitement," Dr. Stern explained. "I woke up around four-thirty and have been in my lab since five o'clock."

Why couldn't Charlie focus on Dr. Stern's words? Since she'd made her claim last night that Armas had traveled through time, she had been anxious for physical evidence to support it. But the revelation about the body, the footprints, and Demarco's strange words and behavior filled her mind.

Could Demarco be the one who murdered the man in the woods?

CHAPTER 8

DR. STERN TOOK the podium and unlocked her case. "Now that we might have additional evidence coming from North Dakota, we will be able to do some comparisons." She removed the two plastic baggies she'd filled with small bits of the boy's clothing and held them up for everyone to see. "I was able to look at the fibers under a microscope earlier this morning. It is most certainly wool. The sample, however, was a coarse wool, not the finer wools we see from merino sheep or even goats. That would be mohair or cashmere. This was a rougher wool. Less processed. The fibers were coarse and the weave rather loose. I made comparisons to some wool items I had at home. The tunic has a very rough texture and appearance. It also appeared to be undyed."

"But you couldn't tell the age of the wool?" asked the chief. His posture was rigid, and his mouth formed a tight line. "For example, did anything about your investigation give you a date? A time in history? Did this come from some other time period or whatever Cutter is claiming?"

Charlie flinched. Why did his accusations sting to much?

"No, I could not age the piece, Chief," Dr. Stern said. "But, if we are accepting that the child travelled through time, the age would not match the amount of time between the fifteenth century and the twenty-first. Armas skipped right over six centuries and so did his clothing."

"The fifteenth century? That's what she's claiming?" Chief Ricard's gaze looked away, and he crossed his arms. "This is nonsense."

"Let's continue, shall we?" Commander Orr said.

"The other aspect of his tunic I examined was the stitching. I wanted to know the quality of the thread, the type of stitching used." Dr. Stern displayed a baggie, which held a one-inch clip of thread. "The thread is wool, handspun. The quality was not very fine, and it was clear that it had been made by hand. I brought a sample of modern thread for the team to examine." She handed Demarco and Kellerman spools of thread. They sat on opposite sides near the head of the conference table. "I will pass around the sample so you can see for yourselves. The difference can be seen with the naked eye, but I can send you my photos when it was under the microscope."

Everyone examined the thread and made a comparison to the sample, except Chief, who slid it across the table to Charlie with an eye roll.

"The only conclusions I can make from my examination is that these are handmade items—the wool cloth used to make the tunic, and the thread used to stitch it together. However, I would need to consult a fibers expert to see if this tunic could be an item from the past. Perhaps a DNA-level test of the wool or an x-ray, which has been used to date fabrics in recent years."

"Thank you, Dr. Stern." Commander Orr took the front of the room once more. "Really we are no further along in determining where—and when—Armas came from." He looked pointedly at Charlie. "However, I think Kellerman's trip to North Dakota might be the very thing we need to prove Petty Officer Cutter's translations of the text are accurate."

Chief snorted.

"Will someone be investigating who murdered this person?" Charlie asked. Why did her voice tremble so? "Everything we learned so far points to foul play."

Demarco repositioned himself in his chair.

Did he have anything to do with it? Her blood ran cold at the thought. The man she'd been with last night bore no resemblance to a ruthless killer. But she had to admit, Angel could be distant, could be sullen. What did she really know about his background? His capabilities?

"I think we are setting the cart before the horse," the commander said. "I'm more interested in the possible connection of the body to the pod at Devils Lake and then the connection to Armas. Once we do those tests, maybe we can talk about why he died or if he was killed."

Didn't he care that someone may have been murdered?

Charlie opened her mouth to speak.

Demarco touched her arm.

She jumped at the unexpected touch. Their gazes met. He had a pained expression on his face, and his eyebrows drew in.

What was he trying to tell her?

Dr. Stern spoke, "I agree with Commander Orr. Let's examine the body, test the DNA, see what we can link together. We can't even begin to think about the how of this person's death before we know who he is."

"I'll make sure I bring everything back, ready to test," Kellerman said. "My contact said the body has been put into a body bag and will be on ice at Minot when I arrive."

"Make sure you take the time to interview the people who found the body." The commander paced at the front of the room. "I want you physically on the scene. Take as many photos as you can. I'd rather have too much to examine, than too little."

"I'd like to request one last time to go with the lieutenant,"

Demarco said quietly. "I thought this is why you brought me on the team."

"As I recall, you wormed your way onto this team last year, Agent," Orr snapped. "Enough already. We have our assignments." The commander scooped up a sheaf of papers on the table and left the podium. "Petty Officer Cutter, would you like to give your presentation now? Kellerman is wheels up in two hours, and I want to give him time to prepare for his flight."

After explaining her theories to the group, everyone except Chief Ricard agreed Charlie's translations coupled with the arrival of Armas supported her theory. The meeting wrapped up, and everyone began to exit the conference room to return to their work.

Chief and Kellerman followed behind Orr.

Dr. Stern carefully packed the baggies into the case.

Charlie had questions for Angel, not the least of which was Orr's accusations about how Angel ended up in A Group, but couldn't ask them freely with the doctor in the room.

Demarco pushed his chair back.

"Wait," Charlie said. "Can you give me five minutes?"

Dr. Stern glanced at them from her position behind the podium. "I'm sorry, am I in the middle of something between you two?"

"There's nothing between us," Demarco said. His fingers drummed out a rhythm on the edge of the conference table.

Charlie froze.

The doctor raised a brow. "Clarissa is a very sweet young lady. If you want to know, I delivered her safely back to her condo last night. She has your painting and told me she was sure you'd be in touch." She snapped her case shut.

He rubbed the back of his neck. "Right. Thanks. That was very kind of you."

Charlie's stomach soured at the reminder. How serious was he about her? He'd left one woman in the middle of a date, and managed to end up in her bed by midnight. A player. Just like Stormy had warned. But, to be honest, she hadn't cared last night either. The attraction between them had been too magnetic. Her curiosity—and her libido—had gotten the better of her.

Dr. Stern glanced past Demarco. "Charlie, I have your painting in my trunk. If you want, you can follow me out to the parking lot, and I can give it to you."

As much as she wanted a few minutes alone with Angel to dig for some answers, she didn't want to be rude. "I suppose I can scoot out for a few minutes."

"Great." The older woman smiled. "That way I hit two birds with one stone this morning. Give me a moment to chat with the commander. I'll meet you out in the lobby."

Demarco remained seated.

As soon as the doctor left, Charlie unloaded. "What is going on, Angel? You said you never saw anyone in the woods, that those footprints were bogus. Why did you lie to me?"

"I don't want to lie to you." His neck muscles jumped under his skin. So much tension beneath the exterior.

"So you admit that you did." Her thoughts went spinning. "I don't understand. If I am part of the team, if Commander Orr is in charge of this office, why are you keeping information hidden? How can I be so sure you didn't have something to do with the death of the man they found in the woods?" If only she could go back to last night, when they were in bed together. Nothing between them. He would've told her just about anything she asked.

"I didn't murder anyone." He flinched as he said the words. "Do you really believe that?"

She pushed up the sleeves of the hoodie she wore. "I don't want to believe it, but the evidence isn't looking good."

"Charlie—" He leaned toward her and touched her knees.

She couldn't keep her gaze off his hands. The warmth burned through her jeans. "Why did you lie to me about the footprints? Let's start there."

"I didn't know if I could trust you." His eyes were a crisp, clear brown.

"Trust me with what?" She bit her thumbnail. "What aren't you telling me?"

Angel rose from his chair and quietly closed the door to the conference room. He leaned against it for a few seconds. "I know who was in the pod."

"What?" A fluttery feeling hit her stomach. "How could you know who was in that pod?" Everything she thought she knew about Angel, who he was, where he came from, what his motives were, were shot down like clay pigeons in a target shoot. "I don't understand you. You aren't making any sense."

His gaze met hers. "I want to tell you everything, I do. But you have to understand, I'm used to being alone, staying in my own head."

The Voynich text returned to her mind. The unbelievable truth she'd found in that manuscript had somehow been easy to accept. It had made sense in a swirl of confusing events and impossible theories. If she had been willing to accept the facts she'd uncovered in the translations, she had to be willing to trust what Angel had to offer. That seemed the fair and right thing to do.

"You can trust me," Charlie said.

His forehead wrinkled. "I'll try."

Charlie sucked in a breath, held it a few seconds, and let it go. Give him a chance to explain. Give him the benefit of the doubt. "How did you know this person?"

"There's so much to tell, Charlie." He rubbed his forehead. "So much."

"That's okay."

"Is it?" In the fluorescent lights, his brown eyes sharpened. He hung back keeping a void between them. "Once I start down this path, there's no turning back. Are you sure you really want the truth?"

CHAPTER 9

CHARLIE AND ANGEL sat silently staring at each other. Was she ready to find out what Angel had been hiding from her—and from the team?

"Yesterday, I wasn't sure anyone would believe my translations nor the fact that I thought Armas had traveled from the past." His support of her theory had buoyed her. How many times had she felt alone translating with no one willing to accept her work? "You trusted me then, so I have to trust you now. Yes, I want the truth, Angel. I need the truth. I want to help you. You don't need to carry this alone anymore."

He closed his eyes. As if an invisible weight had been lifted from his shoulders, the tight muscles in his neck relaxed. "I know who the man was in the pod, because I've seen him before. During an operation gone bad. One that put me in my current position."

"Where did you see him? I don't understand." Orr had indicated Angel had forced himself into A Group. Why? What kind of work had he been doing before last summer?

"I was the lead on a team in charge of tracking down fugitives who had begun experimental work that was dangerous to mankind."

"Experimental?"

"Altering DNA. Human DNA. They wanted to create a superior human being. We couldn't let them."

"Who is 'we'? The federal government? The CIA?"

"The Purists." He stumbled over the words. "We had to stop them."

"I've never heard of that group before...the Purists?" Charlie ran through recent news stories about terrorists and enemies abroad. The name didn't ring a bell.

"There is so much to explain and not enough time. The rest of the team will wonder why we are still in here together." He glanced at the closed door. "But you have to believe I didn't kill that man. I only wanted to track him down and ask him questions. He wasn't someone to fear, but there is another."

"But, Angel, the pods. They're time machines. I still don't understand how you could recognize this person. What are you saying?"

His chest rose and fell. He bit his lip.

Her mind raced. Could Demarco really be the same as Armas? The same as the man in the pod from Devils Lake?

Dr. Stern popped her head inside the room. "Ready to come pick up your painting, Charlie?" A friendly smile lit up her face.

Her stomach churned. She wanted to ask more questions. She wanted more information. Her mind filled in the gaps, and the reality choked her. How was that possible?

"Charlie?" the doctor's question had a lilt of confusion in it.

She snapped back to the normal world. A world where people went to Saturday night painting classes and drank glasses of wine. A world where a daughter fretted over a family dinner she didn't wish to attend, but knew she should. A world where people were born, lived, and died without having any clue about time travel or its implications on world events.

Charlie squeezed Angel's hand. "We need to talk more—later."

He nodded. "I trust you, Charlie."

"I know." She gave him a smile before joining Dr. Stern outside the conference room.

"Looks like you two are getting cozy." The doctor poked Charlie gently in the ribs with her elbow.

Charlie's face grew warm. "Could be." If the doctor only knew the truth of how cozy, which went well beyond the realm of the physical. How soon could she and Angel find time alone for him to share more? An endless supply of questions popped into her mind.

Dr. Stern smiled. "I thought you might be good for him. A man shouldn't be so alone. It's not healthy."

They exited into the hall and headed to the elevators.

"There's a lot more to Angel than I knew." Charlie pushed the 'up' button.

"He's definitely a man of many mysteries." The two women stood shoulder to shoulder waiting on the elevator. "The strong but silent type. Though I'll miss pushing his buttons."

"Why would you stop?" Charlie grinned.

"I like you too much." The doctor patted her on the back. "He's made a good choice for once, and I'm not going to get in the middle of it."

"That's kind of you to say."

They entered the elevator and, as they rose to the lobby, Charlie wondered who exactly she'd fallen for and what other secrets he had to tell.

They strolled in amicable silence through the lobby and outside toward the parking lot.

Dr. Stern knew Commander Orr well and had joined A Group at the beginning. Could she perhaps present a different view of

Angel? It might provide her a foundation for when she found time to question him more thoroughly.

"So how well do you know him?" Good softball question.

"Angel?" Dr. Stern slowed her steps and smiled to herself. "I remember the first day he showed up in the office. He wasn't as confident as he is now. Seemed a little befuddled by some of the office equipment. I thought maybe he'd been out in the field so long that he'd gotten out of the habit. You know the type: all brawn and no brain?"

Charlie nodded. If she interrupted, Abigail might stop talking, and she needed her to keep talking and reveal everything she could about the man.

"Well, he caught on pretty quick, as I recall. Anyway, he and the commander did bump heads a few times. Guess David— Commander Orr—didn't request him for the team. Was surprised when he showed up."

"Oh? How strange."

Dr. Stern shrugged. "People get assigned and reassigned to things all the time in a cleared setting. You know how it goes." She pointed her key fob at her parked vehicle to unlock it. "But he had the paper work, the clearance docs, everything. After a few weeks of working together, David accepted it. And it's worked out rather well. Except for the lost samples—"

"When did that happen?"

The doctor popped the trunk. "Ah, here we are."

Charlie's partially completed painting lay on top of a gym bag. All she'd managed to finish was the basic parts of the owl. Its massive round eyes stared back as if watching her every move.

"I think you did rather well for your first painting class," Abigail remarked. She lifted out the canvas and handed it to Charlie. "My cousin hopes you'll come back for another one, and maybe finish it next time."

Could she imagine herself sitting on a stool painting another garish example of art-gone-wrong? "That would be lovely." She clutched the canvas. Where would she stow it once she returned to the office? "You were saying...about the lost samples?"

Dr. Stern closed the trunk. "Yes, that was really unfortunate. We still don't know what happened to them. David blamed Angel, as he was supposed to be the one in charge of any evidence gathered. It caused a pretty good rift between them for a few weeks. That's sort of why Angel is scared of me." She shook her head. "He knows my relationship with David goes back quite a few years. And because David bumped heads with him at the very start, Angel assumed I would take David's side in everything. I suppose I shouldn't have teased him about things, knowing his view, but it was easy to do. He can be so rigid sometimes, you know? I wanted him to loosen up. Looks like it might've backfired on me."

"Right." Charlie stood awkwardly holding the canvas to her chest. "Well, I guess I need to head back. I have a lot of work ahead of me today. Everything has ramped up so quickly since last night. And with Kellerman heading back to North Dakota—"

Abigail lowered her voice to a whisper and scanned the parking lot. "Can't wait for him to come back with a whole body." She rubbed her hands together. "I'll be buried with work the next few days, too. Just how I like it."

Charlie took a few steps backward. "Thanks again for the canvas."

"My pleasure." The older woman opened the driver's side door and then stopped herself from climbing in. "One more thing, Charlie."

"Yes?" Her stomach fluttered uncomfortably.

"Angel really seems to like you. Different than the other women I've seen him with."

Charlie's cheeks heated.

"Give him a chance. I think there's someone really special under all of that bravado."

Charlie shifted her gaze to a small dent in Abigail's bumper. A ghost of last night crossed through her mind—her body entangled with Angel's. Her heart picked up speed. "I'll keep that in mind."

How could she think of a relationship with a man who'd practically confessed he, too, may have time travelled? Who was Angel Demarco? And where did he come from?

———

When Charlie returned to the office with her owl painting in tow, she spied Angel in the commander's office deep in conversation. She'd have to find a later opportunity to pull him aside and answer more of her questions. On the solitary walk through the parking lot, she'd thought of many new ones.

Kellerman had departed for his flight to North Dakota, and Chief Ricard looked to be knee deep in a pile of radar data from the last twelve months, to ensure they hadn't missed any additional pods.

Charlie sat at her desk and contemplated the possibility Angel had come from a different time. Her mind could barely comprehend it. How could someone from the fifteenth century blend into the twenty-first with almost no one suspecting a thing? He hadn't confessed to it, but he'd implied it with some of what he'd revealed to her earlier. Could he be found in the Voynich text? Or some evidence he was connected to it?

She opened up her work. The colorful pages were familiar yet she saw them in a new light with the recent revelations about Armas and Angel's possible connections to it. She dove into translating every page—from the beginning. A need to understand everything about the text grabbed hold of her like a magnet did an iron filing. The answers were in here somewhere. She knew it. All she needed now was time and focus.

Charlie paused in her analysis. Her eyes burned from staring too long at her computer screen. Tipping her head from one shoulder to the other, she waited for a pain-relieving crack.

"Let me help." Angel gently massaged her neck.

How long had he been behind her?

A flood of heat hit her at the touch of his warm hands. "Wow, you're good at that." Her tight muscles relaxed as he kneaded with his thumbs.

What would her co-workers think about such intimacy between them? But Angel's hands were working miracles on her neck, so why did she care? She closed her eyes and a long sigh escaped her lips.

He leaned down and whispered in her ear, "There's only three of us. Kellerman's gone, Chief finished his analysis, and Orr's making phone calls to Minot."

Her eyes snapped open. Although she wanted to let him continue his massage, which had developed into more of a caress, she had too many questions in her head. She covered one of his hands with hers. "I need more answers."

His hands stilled. "I know."

Did she detect a tremor in his voice? "You said you trusted me. I want to help, but I need to know more."

Her phone vibrated on her desk. A text from her brother.

Crap. What poor timing.

Glancing at the time on her desktop, she knew Angel's story would have to wait. "I have this family dinner to go to." She scooped up her phone.

Beep, beep! I'm outside.

"My brother's picking me up, and it looks as if he's early." She flashed her phone screen so he could see the text.

Angel's unblinking gaze unnerved her. Then he slowly nodded. "Right. Family. I understand."

No way was she going to give Angel the chance to clam up. She'd finally gotten him talking, and a family dinner wasn't going to get in the way of finding out the answers she needed. "How about we meet tonight when I get back? Before we're back in the office with interruptions and assignments and—" She glanced at Orr still busy in his office. "Other people."

He bit his lip and searched her face. "All right. Tonight. I'll pick you up?"

She nodded. "I'll text you when my brother drops me off."

He gave her a slight smile and took a few steps back. "Okay. I'll explain everything. Tonight. I promise."

"If I can handle pods falling from the sky and a time traveling boy, I'm sure anything you have to tell me can't be any worse."

Angel gestured at her phone. "You'd better answer him before he starts wondering where you are."

"Right." She tapped on the phone screen and quickly texted Chad to wait a few minutes.

Angel retreated, heading toward the door.

"Wait, I wanted to share something with you." How could she forget? He'd been so interested in her translation work and what else she might find. Although a majority of the deciphering revealed mysterious formulas and plant biology, she'd uncovered something intriguing.

He approached her desk.

"I think I found another name." She clicked through the Voynich pages she'd been working on. "Right here. A signature, I think."

"Show me." Angel's voice shook.

She enlarged the page with a few clicks. "See here? Ree-sa. A name. Do you think this could be Armas's mother?"

In a daze, Angel knelt next to her and touched the name on the screen. "Risa. Oh, my God. It can't be true."

CHAPTER 10

CHARLIE'S BODY TENSED. "You know that name?"

Angel scrubbed a hand over his face. "I imagined it was possible, but I hoped I was wrong." He stared down at his lap. "I never should have done it. Never."

"Done what? Who's Risa?" She grew lightheaded. Thoughts swirled in her mind. None of this made any sense. How could she leave to meet her brother when Angel had just confessed he knew the name she'd uncovered?

He winced. "I'll explain everything, Charlie. I will." His usual resonant voice weakened to a thin whisper.

Commander Orr's booming voice interrupted them both. "It's five o'clock. I think we've done enough for today. I'd like to lock up."

"Right. Five o'clock." Angel stood and stepped away from Charlie as if in a daze. "You need to go meet your brother, Cutter."

"You have plans, Petty Officer?" Orr ignored the strange actions of his security specialist and focused in on Charlie.

"Just a family dinner." How could she possibly set aside what she'd learned about Risa and Angel and pretend everything was normal at her parents' house? The idea of it was ridiculous. Impossible. Not doable.

"Delightful. Families are important, wouldn't you agree, Demarco?" Orr clapped him on the back.

Angel's shoulders curved inward. "Yes, sir, very important." He couldn't meet Charlie's eyes.

"Well, let's skedaddle then. I'll lock up behind you." Orr pointed at Charlie's computer. "Shut that down, and let's go."

"Yes, sir." Charlie saved her work and turned off her desktop.

The two men made their way to the door. To anyone who didn't know him, Angel appeared steady, quiet, and thoughtful. But Charlie noticed the stumble in his step, the weakness in his profile. As if all the bravado and rigidity had been sucked out of him.

After she shut off her monitor, she followed them into the hall. Her questions would have to wait.

———

Chad honked on his horn three times in a row when he saw his sister approaching.

She jumped at the noise, her mind still buried in thought.

Her brother leaned across the passenger's seat and popped open the door. "Hurry up! We're going to be late."

"Sorry." Charlie slid in and closed the door of her brother's Honda. "I had to work today."

"Work?" He scanned her casual outfit. "Since when do Navy linguists wear civvies to the office?"

"It's Sunday."

"So?"

"We're a mixed office—some civilian, some military. It has a different dress code."

"If I were the Officer-in-Charge—"

"You're not, okay? Commander Orr is in charge, and what he says goes. He has zero problems with me wearing this." Why did she let her temper get the best of her? Chad didn't know the bizarre details of her job and her personal life and how they were mixing together in a very uncomfortable and confusing way, but he could sometimes be a bit of an annoyance.

The good brother. The obedient brother. He was the boy her father always wanted; she was the girl her father always butted heads with.

Tonight's dinner at her parent's house was to celebrate Chad's new orders, his career taking off, the amazing responsibilities he'd have...and no one would know anything about what she was working on, nor how important it was. Regular military life seemed so boring and trite in comparison to the truths she encountered in merely one week at her new assignment. Pods, time travelers, a boyfriend who may be a time traveler...who may even be connected to the death of another time traveler.

Chad snapped his fingers in front of her eyes. "Hey, sis, where did you go? I thought you were about to give me a royal thrashing, and you just disappeared there. Hello! Earth to Charlene."

She slapped his hand away. "It's been a long week, okay? Let's go. If you're so worried about being late, let's drive. The traffic can't be that terrible on a Sunday afternoon, can it?"

Chad let his hand drop. "Fine." He drove toward the beltway and their parent's place in Columbia, a high-end suburb between Baltimore and Washington D.C.

Charlie had only visited once before. Halfway through her second year of grad school, her mother had bought her a plane ticket for Christmas. Her father had received new orders from Texas to the National Security Agency on Fort Meade twelve months earlier. Not exactly a family home to her. But most military brats lived similarly—constantly on the move, always starting over, unpacking, repacking. Lather, rinse, repeat.

"Have you found out yet whether you can live off-base?" Chad smoothly transitioned to a different topic. If he ever got married, he'd know exactly how to handle a wife in a prickly mood.

"Should find out soon." She stared out the car window at the stuttering traffic—stop, go, stop, go. The traffic in D.C. never seemed to improve no matter what time of day or night. "Rumor has it they don't have any space in the barracks for another female sailor."

"Hope you can find a decent apartment. Pricey around there." Chad flicked on his signal for a few seconds and merged like Jeff Gordon on the Talledega Speedway to make the exit ramp for 95.

Charlie gripped her seat. "I'd like to make it to Mom and Dad's in one piece, please."

He snorted. "Everyone drives like that around here."

Her mind flashed to last night when Angel had almost run them into the orange barrels on the way to the pod. How similar these two men were. "Are we really in that much of a hurry for Mom's meatloaf?"

"She making ham." Chad ran a hand through his short, brown hair. "I know Dad can get under your skin, but can I ask you to just lay off tonight?"

"He doesn't get under my skin."

Her brother gave her the side eye. "Yeah, right." He sped up to pass a minivan that had slowed down for a merging vehicle. "For Mom's sake, let's keep the topic of conversation on easy stuff."

"Like?"

"The food, the weather, her latest knitting project—"

"Mom's knitting again?" Charlie had a hard time holding back a laugh.

"Yeah," Chad said with a smile. "Prepare for all of your Christmas presents this year to be 'handmade' yarn nightmares. She's been taking a class at some yarn shop near their house."

She could do this. She could forget for a few hours the weight of the knowledge she held. Chad was right. Talk about easy stuff. Silly stuff. Things that didn't matter. Anything but Angel Demarco and his mysterious background.

———

Charlie fiddled with the radio finding nothing but cheesy pop music, bro country, or static. Light conversation had dropped off. Any minute her brother was going to ask about it. She could sense it. Just like she always could. Almost as if she could hear the gears of Chad's mind cranking through his questions and curiosities about her. When had there been a time in her life without this odd twin connection? She couldn't remember.

"Shut that thing off, would you?" Chad brushed her hand away from the dial. "If you really want to listen to something decent, I have loads of good music." He paired his phone with the car stereo system, and the interior filled with an acoustic guitar cover of 'Hungry Like the Wolf.'

Settling in the passenger's seat, she stared out the window at the lush green shrubbery that lined the freeway. "I feel as if I'm being hijacked."

"Hijacked?" Chad's brows came together. "If you don't like my music, that's fine. We can drive in complete stupid silence for thirty minutes." He tapped on his phone's screen.

"That's not what I meant." Crap, a few days before her brother would be heading to Europe, and she had to step in it. "The dinner. Mom and Dad—"

"This isn't about them. You can't BS me, Char. You've always butted heads with Dad. What's really bugging you?" He poked her side. "What is it you don't want Mom and Dad to know?"

Charlie shrugged. Damn, Chad, and his spidey senses.

He mocked a shocked face—round eyes, open mouth, a hand to his cheek. "Wait, are you seeing someone?"

Her whole body flushed. "Maybe." Her mind already skipped ahead to later that night, a rendezvous with the sexy agent, and a chance to question him more deeply about his past. How did Demarco manage to equally attract and fascinate her?

"Who's the lucky guy?" he asked.

They drove right by the exit for Fort Meade. A sign read: NSA Restricted Entrance. The National Security Agency lay less than a mile from 95. A regular-looking office building stood surrounded by trees and, ever since 9/11, a very solid infrastructure of fences and gates and guarded access points.

Her heart thumped in her chest. Their samples were somewhere inside that facility. Right now, people were possibly analyzing the blood taken from the North Dakota pod site. So tantalizingly close to answers about Armas, the body in the woods, and more.

"Well?" Chad prompted her.

She snapped back to the conversation. "A co-worker."

"God, I hope he's not an officer," he muttered.

Of course that would be his biggest concern: an enlisted person dating an officer. Chad rigidly adhered to military rules and standards without question. When had he not followed every directive ever given to him by parent, teacher, or coach? "No worries, Chad, I'm not dating one of your peers. You're safe from scrutiny."

"That's not what I—" His shoulders bunched up. "I've just seen some really bad outcomes when you cross ranks like that. It's not worth it. No matter how great the guy is. It's a mess not worth getting into."

The tone of his voice made her wonder if perhaps Chad was not such a rigid rules follower after all. A personal experience with an enlisted woman, perhaps? Something to ponder.

"I'll take that into consideration if the opportunity ever comes my way." She carefully controlled her voice to correct him, "His name is Angel Demarco. He's the head of security in our office. Non-military. Which would make you happy, I would think."

"Angel, huh? Sounds like a movie star name."

She chuckled—although the special agent did have the body of a leading man. "He's different."

Chad chewed on that description for a few moments. "So he's not a quiet, librarian type who hangs on your every word?"

"What?"

"Every guy you've ever dated has been such a wimp. Like, absolute loser material."

"And your girlfriends have been perfect?" A few of the women he dated ran through her mind. "Remember Erin? Tall, brunette, and bratty."

"Bratty?" he said with a laugh.

"A girl knows—" Erin had been annoying and clingy and horrible. When her brother had ended that relationship a few years ago, Charlie had let out a joyous shout at the dinner table—when her brother had been ripped to shreds over the break-up. "And I'm sorry she dumped you."

"She didn't dump me."

"Yes, she did. She specifically texted you those words: I, Erin, dump you, Chad."

"I don't remember it quite like that." He stared ahead at the road.

"She broke up with you in a text. That part is true."

"Okay, how did you turn this around on me?" he asked. "I am supposed to be grilling you about your angelic boyfriend."

"His name is Angel. He can't help what his name is." Or could he? If it was true that he was a time traveler, would he have been able to use his given name? Or would he have to take on a new identity to blend into modern society? She sobered at the thoughts that ran through her head. Who was Angel really?

Chad took an exit off of 95 toward their parents' home. "You have exactly five minutes to tell me everything about him or I'll let Mom know."

His teasing took her mind off her speculations. "You wouldn't."

"Do you really want to risk finding out?" He waggled his eyebrows.

She crossed her arms in faux outrage. "Fine." Didn't she deep down want to tell someone about Angel? He was one part mystery, one part hunk. A man who challenged her, confounded her, and attracted her. A dangerous combination. "I'll tell you about him. But no mention of him at Mom and Dad's."

Chad raised a hand. "I swear."

"Sweetheart!" Angela Cutter enveloped her daughter in a warm hug. She smelled like fresh-baked bread and merlot. "You're wasting away to nothing." With a firm grip, she held her daughter a foot away to examine her head to toe. "Are you eating three meals a day?"

"Yes, mom, I'm eating." Charlie didn't tell her mother she also was obsessively swimming in the evenings to burn off nervous energy and clear her head. "You rearranged the living room."

"That was months ago." Her mother stepped away to give her brother a similar greeting. "Tall, dark, and handsome. I'm sure all the girls have googly eyes for you, honey."

"Mom." Chad's face reddened. "I'm almost twenty-six. You make it sound as if I'm still in the seventh grade."

Angela shook off the criticism and locked arms with her twin children. "Harrison, the kids are here. Time to be social."

Daisy, the aging and prickly family cat, rubbed against Charlie's legs and meowed.

Charlie's mother marched her and her brother into the dining room and pointed to a seat on the left side of the table. "You sit here, Charlie."

A decorative ceramic platter filled the middle of the table laden with steaming roast beef.

"I thought you said we were having ham?" Charlie shot an accusatory look at her brother who took his seat opposite her.

"Ham?" Her mother trilled her usual high pitched laugh. "Your father hates ham. Too salty or something. I can never remember."

As much as Charlie loved her happy-go-lucky, absentminded mother, her inattention to detail sometimes landed her in hot water with her husband and her children.

Captain Harrison Cutter entered from the opposite doorway. "I love ham. I can't stand lamb. Ham, lamb. Hmmm." He kissed his wife on the cheek before taking a seat at the head of the table.

"That's right." Angela stamped her foot. "Ah, but everyone loves roast beef. I can never go wrong with a roast." She sat in the last empty chair opposite her husband.

"Charlene, you are looking well." Her father eyed her up and down before pouring himself a glass of the merlot on the table.

Her mother must have decided to take a nip before dinner.

"Thanks." She waited for the criticisms to begin. One compliment was typically followed by a barrage of comments that made her feel worse than when she walked in the door.

Chad, perhaps wanting to avoid the usual arguments, interrupted, "Let's eat. I'm starving. Everything looks delicious."

Their mother beamed. "It's only the usual stuff. I'm sure they feed you well in the officer's mess."

Chad took a heaping serving of carved roast beef and then passed the platter to their father. "The food's okay, but I'm going to miss home cooking."

"Rota. You must be excited about that assignment." Harrison Cutter scooped out mashed potatoes on his plate. "I always hoped to go back overseas."

"Sweetheart," said Angela. "For the kids' sake I'm so glad you were able to stay stateside for the most part." She poured herself a fresh glass of wine.

Wasn't that quite of bit of drinking for her mother? In the past, the woman couldn't finish half a glass.

Her mother redirected the conversation, "Charlie, can you tell us anything about your change in orders? That was so sudden and unusual, wouldn't you say, dear?" She gave her husband a pointed look from across the table.

"I don't know, Mom." Her stomach dipped. Why did she feel so uncomfortable discussing the topic? Anticipating negativity?

"Well, you needed your research, so they must've found out about your studies. Is that it?" Her mother forked a slice of beef and set it on her plate. "That weird manuscript you gave up on."

"I didn't give up." Charlie stopped mid-bite, a spoonful of peas in the air.

"Well, you quit the program," her father said. "Not sure how else we are supposed to perceive that except 'giving up.'"

"Right," Charlie snapped. "I'm a quitter and a failure, I forgot."

"I never said—" Her father raised his voice.

Chad held up a hand. "Can we eat in peace, please? My God, you two ruin every nice meal with this shit."

"Chad, your language," Angela Cutter admonished.

"Sorry, Mom, but how can you stand it?" When he set down his fork, it clanged against the china plate. "I wanted one nice night with all of you before I ship out for the next three years, and they couldn't do it. Not for me. Not even for you, Mom."

Charlie lowered her eyes and pushed her peas around her plate. Why couldn't she control her temper? She had mentally fortified herself for tonight and had failed miserably. "Sorry, Chad."

"I never said you were a failure." Her father quietly cut into a slice of beef. "But something made you leave school and join the Navy without telling us anything. I wish you would've asked for some input."

"Harrison," her mother hissed.

Spots of color appeared in Chad's face. He pushed back from the table. "Just stop it. I don't know why the two of you always go at it like rabid dogs, but I'm sick of it. Dad: Charlie is an adult and can make decisions without your input. Charlie: Dad is only worried about you and wants the best for you." He gripped the back of his chair until his knuckles turned white. "There. Can we move on?"

"Honey, please, sit down." Angela Cutter's eyes grew watery, and she reached for her son. "Please." Her posture crumpled.

Harrison Cutter stood up from the table and set his napkin on his plate, "I've lost my appetite."

"Dad, come on," Chad said.

Their father lifted a hand to wave off his son's plea and retreated to his office at the back of the house.

Angela Cutter dropped her chin. "He loves you so much, Charlie."

"Oh, Mom." What was it about her father that set her off so much? Although she desperately wanted his approval, she never seemed to be able to live up to his expectations. Every choice a mistake. Every opinion wrong.

"You're just too much alike." Her mother took a drink of wine. "That's what I've always said." As she stared out the front window behind her husband's chair, her gaze blurred.

Chad walked over to his mother and put an arm around her shoulders. "That's it, Mom. And they both can't see it." He locked eyes with Charlie and nodded his head.

She gulped. She knew what he meant, and because she loved her mother and hated to see her so distraught, she said, "I'm dating someone, Mom."

Her mother sniffed a few times, squeezed her son's hand, and lifted her head. "Oh? Tell me about him. Is he handsome?"

CHAPTER 11

"HARRY, THE KIDS LEFT." Angela stood in the doorway of her husband's study. "I wish you'd joined us for dessert."

He sat in his favorite chair next to a side table with a single reading lamp lit and a book in his lap. "Charlene knows." How that was possible he didn't know, but deep inside he'd felt it for a while. "We should've told them a long time ago."

"No." Angela's reply was sharp and tinged with fear. "That's not true. She was only annoyed with you, as per usual. Ever since high school, you two have butted heads. This is nothing different. When two people are so much alike—"

He slammed the book shut. "Stop it, Angie. Just stop it. Why do you insist on that kind of nonsense?" With a flourish, he whipped off his reading glasses and knit his brows.

His wife shrank back. "I only meant that you both have so much in common: stubborn, smart, determined."

"Yes, Charlene's always been smart. Too smart for her own good." He smiled at the memory of his daughter as a young girl winning every science fair and spelling bee she entered. But his heart sank at the adult Charlene. Slipping away from them. Becoming someone he didn't recognize. "And she knows that something isn't right about this family."

Angela's eyes grew wet. "How dare you say that, Harrison."

He rose from his chair and placed his book back on the wall of bookshelves behind his desk. "I didn't say that to hurt you, Angie."

"Our family is just as normal as anyone else's."

With tender hands, he gripped his wife's narrow shoulders. "Of course it is, sweetheart. But someday we will have to tell them. And I'd rather choose that moment than have Charlene figure it out by herself. That would be so much worse."

Angela looked up at him. "Can't it wait a little while longer?" Her face grew red and splotchy. "She was opening up to me out there. Telling me about a man she's dating. I don't want to drive her away." She wiped the back of her hand across her nose.

Her pleading words drove a knife into his heart. How could he hurt his beautiful wife? How could he ruin the relationship she had with her twin children by confessing their deepest secrets? Secrets husband and wife had promised to keep between them forever?

But neither one of them had known when they'd looked down at baby Charlene and baby Chad snuggled together in a single crib that someday those babies would grow up and have minds of their own. That they might wonder about things that didn't add up. Questions people asked. Timelines that didn't quite match up with the dates.

He pointed to a framed photograph on the wall of his study. "Remember when they were little? It was so much easier then."

Angela turned to view the photo of Charlene and Chad as toddlers washing their old German Shepherd, Duke, with the hose in the backyard of their base housing in Texas. Charlene had a thousand-watt smile on her face and held the hose, while Chad scrubbed the dog down with a sponge he'd found in the laundry room.

His wife smiled, but the smile didn't reach her eyes. "I sent that to you when you were on TDY in Germany."

"I wish I'd been there for that."

"I know." She put her arm around her husband's waist. "You've been a good father to them. A good provider."

He kissed his wife on the top of her head. Oh, how he wished he'd been there for all the little things. His heart squeezed painfully. "At least I got that part right."

"Maybe we can take a trip to Spain to see Chad when he's all settled in."

Casually, the conversation had shifted away from his desires to be honest with his children to his wife's need to live in her fantasy world a little longer. Where her daughter and son came over for family dinners, and they pretended all was normal, all was fine. And that no secrets existed. How many more years could he remain silent?

As Charlene drifted further away, he had an urgency to confess. He loved his daughter, but the lies were eating at him a little bit at a time. The arguments, the abrasive responses, all a means to protect himself when Charlene found out everything. Would she see him in a different light? A negative light? Would she want to have nothing to do with him? The thought of it was frightening, as she and Chad were his only children, but he knew his daughter sensed it. Deep inside she knew something wasn't right.

"Sure, we can go to Spain after my retirement. In fact, we can go anywhere you've ever wanted to travel, Angie." He drew her into his arms and rested his chin on her head. "All those years you sat at home and waited for me to be free of my obligations? Now it's your turn."

"Harry, I love you so very much." His wife whispered into his chest. "What would I have done without you?"

"I love you, too, Angie."

Without him wanting it to, doubt crept into his mind. Would his wife have chosen him if things had been different? Even after twenty-five years, the idea still plagued him. Would she really?

He tamped down the thought for the millionth time and hugged his wife closer.

CHAPTER 12

CHARLIE WAVED at her brother as he sat idling his car on the curb near Angel's apartment. Although she was grateful he'd agreed to drop her off at the special agent's home, the protective brother thing needed to end. Guess he wasn't going to leave until he saw her safely enter the building. If her brother could see her face, he'd notice the most exaggerated eye roll in the history of eye rolls.

How embarrassing. As if Chad were her father, and she was going on a date to prom.

Before she could knock, Angel opened the door wearing a loose pair of athletic pants and a gray t-shirt that clung to his well-developed chest and shoulders.

"Is that your brother?" Angel stood barefoot on the stoop and squinted at the dark vehicle lurking on the street.

Charlie shielded her eyes and looked down at the concrete path in front of his apartment. "Is he still there?" Why did her ears feel so hot?

He gently grasped her by the shoulders and moved her three inches to his right. "Yes. Should I ask him to come in?"

"God, no." Her heart skipped a beat.

He chuckled. "I'm kidding, Charlie." Instead of approaching her brother's car, Angel gave a quick wave at the tinted windows.

Chad sped off.

"Thank God." She drew a deep breath through her nose. "Dinner was brutal."

"Oh?" He guided her inside. "Tell me more."

The air smelled of wet potting soil and fertilizer. Could it be possible Angel had added another three or four plants to his collection since her first visit?

"My mother knows all about you, which means—" She checked the time on her cell phone. "So does my father by now. Expect to be asked to some sort of awkward dinner at a chain restaurant in the near future with Angela and Harrison. My mother loves the Olive Garden. I pre-apologize."

He raised a brow. "Sounds interesting."

Angel spun her to face him in the foyer. Their gazes met.

"Hello," she breathed. His brown eyes glowed and held a warmth she'd only recently noticed.

"Hello," he whispered.

While his hands clasped her waist, he kissed her slowly.

After the stressful evening at her parent's home, the close contact soothed her and brought down the tension inside. Could she forget about the questions she had and, instead, spend the evening in his arms? Vivid memories of the previous night filled her mind. Wouldn't be so bad to experience a repeat performance.

They broke apart.

He swept a hand across her brow. "You are so beautiful."

Heat crept into her cheeks. They were getting way off track. "Thanks." She pulled out of his grasp.

"Something wrong?" His hands remained suspended in the air, as if he held a ghost Charlie in them.

Crap. She'd messed up.

"I'm sorry, I didn't mean to be so abrupt." She rubbed a hand over her lips. "I have so many questions for you, and I didn't want us to get—you know—*distracted*."

He nodded his head slowly. "You're right. You're right." His gaze roved her figure. I just can't help myself." He slipped past her, touching her hip, and headed to the kitchen. "Do you want a drink? Tea? Coffee?"

She took a seat in the brown armchair. "Some coffee would be great."

"You got it."

As he searched in his cupboard for coffee and a filter, Charlie made light conversation as a warm up to the harder questions she wanted to ask. "I wish I had a green thumb like you. I had a cactus once, a gift from a friend, and I managed to kill it in one semester. Something about too much water, or not enough water? Wait, don't cactus like no water? I can't remember."

"Cactuses need water, but not very much." Angel filled the reservoir of the coffeemaker with fresh water from the tap. "I grew up around plants. I guess it's rote for me now. I don't even think about it. I put them on a watering schedule, fertilizer, and those lights up there." He pointed at several can lights that were mounted in the ceiling above her. "Full-spectrum day bulbs. Whenever I go to work, I turn them on."

"Quite the set up. I probably couldn't handle more than one."

"I could point you in the right direction, if you really wanted to try again. Although you wouldn't think it, orchids are very easy to care for." He pointed at a cluster of blooming orchids in one corner of the room—pink, white, yellow. "Especially in such a humid climate. They love humidity. We didn't have orchids where I grew up. It was one of the first plants I acquired when I moved in here. So delicate and special. My mother would've loved them." His gaze grew unfocused, and his posture relaxed.

"Tell me more about where you grew up." The tenderness in his voice surprised her. "And when you grew up. I want to know everything."

"One thing at a time, Charlie. One thing at a time." He pressed the 'on' button on the coffeemaker and then joined her in the living room, choosing a padded wooden bench surrounded by flora of all kinds for his seat. "Let's start with the life I used to live. A life that I probably will never return to." He stared down at his hands for a few moments, as if gathering the courage to speak.

Charlie held her breath and leaned forward. At last, the real story about Angel Demarco and who he really was. "Please," Charlie urged. "Tell me more. I want to know."

Angel looked at his hands and then stroked his chin. "This is hard for me, I want you to understand that."

"You can trust me."

He locked eyes with her and nodded. "There's so much to explain. And a lot of it probably will make no sense."

Charlie clasped her hands together in her lap. "I know you traveled through time and that you had to have traveled in a pod. I know that sometimes you blend in perfectly with everyone around you, and then suddenly you don't. I know that something painful happened and it would feel better if you shared that pain with someone."

He winced. "I don't even know where to start."

"Start at the beginning," she said as calmly as she could.

"The beginning. Yes, the beginning." He let out a sigh. "The truth is, Charlie, I don't know 'when' I grew up, because our idea of time and years have changed over the centuries. But I do know this: I am from a future time. A time well beyond the one we live in now."

"Wait, the future?" Not the answer she had expected. The manuscript, the instructions to build the machine, the arrival of Armas—she'd assumed all of it had occurred hundreds of years ago. She shook her head. "I don't understand. How—?"

"Where I come from, we don't live like you do. All of those gadgets and screens and things."

"But you said you are from a future time." She frowned. "How could that be?"

"We lost knowledge. I didn't realize how much knowledge until I found myself here. And it was overwhelming." His eyes widened before he reasserted control. "The amount of information that zips across the world in a matter of moments. I still sometimes have trouble grasping the concept."

"How was knowledge lost?" She tilted her head to one side.

"We called it the 'Zhadan.' Hundreds of years before my birth." He gestured with his hands, an invisible ball between them, that suddenly flew apart. "A massive weapon of some kind that destroyed all knowledge. All electronics. The whole of the world was knocked down to its knees."

"Who would do such a thing?" She recoiled at the thought.

"We didn't know." He shook his head. "We lived in the aftermath, and life was different for us than our ancestors. We had stories passed down from one generation to the next, and a new written record, but very little survived."

How could that be possible? The millions of texts and journals and newspapers, the learning built upon centuries of tradition and accumulated knowledge. "But you had books, surely, historical texts to rely on."

"No. The books you have on your shelves, the libraries? Before the Zhadan everything had been moved into electronic form after an academic purge sparked by out-of-control mobs. Those in academia and the government decided knowledge was safer in electronic form. They thought they were helping knowledge survive, instead they made it more vulnerable. Only a few books remained as historical pieces for display. Why spend the time and money to print more books when everyone gathered knowledge from electronic sources?"

"How far into the future was this?" Charlie mused.

"I'm not sure." He shrugged. "It could be five hundred years; it could be a thousand. But the exact number doesn't matter, does it?"

"No, I suppose it doesn't."

"So as a result of this disjointed understanding of history, I grew up in a world where electronics were shunned. It was a weakness that had been exploited in the past and returned us to primitive living. We worked hard for everything we had. I grew up in a farming community. We raised pigs and cows and sheep. We ate what we grew. Any attempt to improve our standard of living created fear among the older generations. They'd been raised to maintain a simple lifestyle to avoid a second Zhadan. We couldn't survive another. Great fear surrounded that possibility. We do not know who destroyed the world, so there was fear it could easily happen again."

"Zhadan," Charlie mused. "That sounds familiar." She tucked it away in her mind for further contemplation at a later time. As a logophile, she couldn't turn off that part of her brain. "But how did you travel here if your culture didn't allow for such projects? A machine that travels through time would be more than an 'improvement.' It would require great knowledge and skill."

"Like the mysterious person in the fifteenth century?" he posited.

"Yes. True." As she contemplated the connection between the future and the past, she had a feeling Angel would connect these two things for her if only she could be patient. So much to learn. So much to comprehend. "Another time period with no modern knowledge, yet someone achieved an unheard of marvel."

"Charlie, I mentioned how I lived, how I grew up. As time went on, not everyone accepted our way of life."

"Oh?" Her pulse quickened.

"Most of us wished for humanity to remain pure, unadulterated by unnatural things."

"Like computers, the internet, electricity, even?"

"Yes."

"That sounds so primitive."

"But it worked for us," Angel explained. "We lived a simple life, and though it was hard and sometimes we suffered through difficult times, we persevered as a people."

"It sounds like the Pilgrims."

"By what I have read over the years, it would be similar to the lives of American in the Wild West. Wagon trains, raising cattle, growing crops."

"And who were the other people who wanted to live differently?"

"Eventually they became known as the Genesis Project."

———

Charlie found herself fascinated by the story Angel told. He was from the future, but yet the future was not the world she anticipated it would be. "Why was the Genesis Project different?"

"The Genesis Project began with noble intentions. We'd lost what you'd call 'modern science' after the Zhadan. Many died after that event. Humans had become so dependent on machines and electronics that when they were wiped out, so was everything on which life had been built. Including medical knowledge and scientific advancements. The Genesis Project was a group of our most curious, our most intelligent men and women who grew tired of being held back by our elders and the ruling classes who would not allow for a return to how people before us had once lived."

She couldn't shut off her curious mind from wanting more of an explanation about what had happened to send human beings back to an agrarian lifestyle. Only one thing kept popping up in her mind. "The Zhadan sounds as if it was possibly an EMP—an electromagnetic pulse."

Angel nodded. "I have run across that term since I arrived here, and it does seem to match up with the stories we were told."

"That would fry everything...even down to the components in your car." Charlie considered the implications. "We would definitely be reduced to a primitive state." Factories, power production, trucks, ships, planes—everything upon which the world depended had ended overnight. Her mind reeled at the idea.

"When I was nineteen or twenty, we had an incredibly hard winter." Angel paused here. His shoulders drooped. "Most of our animals died. And because we lost our animals, we had trouble planting crops. There was talk of starvation and difficult times ahead." He stared at nothing, his eyes blank of expression. He crossed his arms as if warding off a terrible memory. "A man came to our village, his name was Byron Allwood. He was part of the Genesis Project. He wanted to recruit more to his cause. He wanted to build an even better world than what existed before the Zhadan. He even spoke of avoiding the mistakes of the past. Many of us were swayed by his arguments." He spat out the last sentence. "When you are cold, hungry, and broken, you can easily be manipulated by words. He urged us to come to a speech he would make the following night in a village not far from us. Both my younger sister and I decided to attend. My parents wouldn't have let us go if they'd known—we were barely out of our teens."

"You have a sister?"

"Yes, I did." He scrubbed a hand over his face. "And I wish I'd never taken her with me. Things would be so different now."

Angel left the bench and returned to the kitchen to pour them each a cup of coffee. He handed her a steaming mug, and Charlie sipped it slowly contemplating the unbelievable story he told. If she hadn't translated the text and seen Armas arrive in a pod with her own eyes, she'd think he was crazy. She wanted to know how this story of the future and his life there tied into the pods and into their research, but needed more details about this mysterious rudimentary existence that awaited mankind many centuries in the future.

"Tell me about the speech," she prompted.

"Allwood explained his plan and the experiments the Genesis Project had been conducting in secret. All animal cells and human cells maintain a small electric charge in order to communicate within the body...brain cells, nerve cells, a whole host of cells. Byron posited that the way to protect the future from another Zhadan would be to create biologic systems using the same principles. Such small electric impulses could not be as easily disrupted. His theories made a lot of sense based off of what we knew about the past. Although my parents hadn't attended his speech, several elders from our village had been curious. The Genesis Project had begun to distill the idea into a working concept, which would rebuild the world to the modern, advanced place it used to be without the risk."

"So did the Genesis Project convince people?" Charlie leaned forward. "Did they have a viable solution?"

"Many of us believed so. Byron Allwood was a convincing speaker. He recruited able bodied men and women to join the work they were involved in. He promised we would all benefit from the discoveries being made. We believed in him—or most of us did. My sister more strongly than myself." His chin dipped to his chest.

Something bad had happened to his sister. She could sense it in his words and body language, but she didn't want to ask. Not yet. She had to let the story play out.

"When the elders found out what Byron and his followers were planning, they were frightened," he continued. "They were worried what this meant for the tenuous existence of human beings in the world. We were facing a bad year with little food, and it was believed wasting time and energy on risky experiments threatened everyone. It used precious resources we didn't have. And that is when the split occurred."

"A split?"

"Between those who wanted a purity of nature, and those who wanted to enhance nature and build an even better world and a better mankind to go with it. Byron called us 'The Purists,' as if it was a dirty name."

"I can understand why many were scared of trying something new."

"Not only trying something new," Angel's voice cranked up a few notches. "We 'Purists' feared altering nature would damage the earth, human beings, animals. We wanted laws in place to stop the Genesis Project devotees from conducting their experiments."

"But how could these experiments be so harmful? Biological circuits? It doesn't sound harmful."

Angel curled his lip. "This is where you are wrong, Charlie. It wasn't merely about recreating circuitry and electronics. I wish it were. But, to convince others their work was good for the world, the Genesis Project began using their new knowledge to experiment genetically on human beings who were considered 'mistakes'—the deformed, the diseased, the insane."

"What kinds of genetic experiments?"

"They hated to see suffering. Disease, physical ailments, injuries. One of these Genesis Project followers managed to find an old medical textbook, long thought lost to time and the elements. It became their Bible. They began to learn from it and had a desire to fix what they saw as needless pain, needless death. And I have to say I think at the beginning, they thought they had a noble cause. But then the Genesis Project followers began experiments we considered going against nature itself. They wanted to be able to correct the 'defects' of humans."

"What defects?"

"Whatever they deemed to be 'wrong' about someone...their appearance, their imperfections."

"I see."

"We Purists saw every human being as worthy and special—from the youngest to the oldest, from the sickest to the healthiest. All had worth and value and were made as they should be."

"But what if you could fix a physical problem with a little bit of knowledge?"

"We didn't see it that way. We all took care of one another, no matter the difficulty. We all cared for each other the same. The

Genesis Project made people feel as if they were damaged, unworthy, in need of correction. And eventually they went beyond merely 'fixing' what was broken. They thought they could make human beings even better."

"Better how?"

CHAPTER 13

ANGEL COULDN'T KEEP STILL. He set his mug on the bench and began to pace the living room, rubbing a hand on the back of his neck. "His work went beyond the norms of humanity...if one person ran fast, Allwood wanted him to run faster. If one person was quick at learning, Allwood wanted to make him even smarter."

"All using genetics? DNA?" Charlie's gaze followed his movements. "But how? You said you had been reduced to a simplistic life. That everything we see around us in the twenty-first century was alien to you and unbelievable."

"These were secrets Allwood kept close to the vest." Angel shrugged. "But we saw the results of his experimentation—the physical and mental ruination of vulnerable human beings, and to what end? Who was this improvement for? Beyond trying to improve how we lived our lives, Allwood seemed bent on an improved human."

"That sounds horrific." Images of the Nazis and their medical experiments on Jews and others in their clutches ran through her mind. History repeating itself, even hundreds of years into the future.

"Some in my village actually sought him out for help with their own ailments or perceived imperfections. He had an ability to hone in on people's weaknesses and convince them he could help." He paused his steps and stared down at his empty hands. "One morning I woke to do my chores in the barn, when it was discovered my own sister had run off to join the Genesis Project."

A sudden coldness hit her core.

Gently, between his fingers, he rubbed a leaf on a rubber plant beside the bench. His voice dropped several notches. "I had no idea Risa had been swayed by Allwood's speeches."

"Risa—" She lifted a hand to her mouth. It couldn't be. His sister?

"She bought into his ideas and had kept it from me, her own brother." His gaze became unfocused. "I thought we had been close. That we shared everything. I was the one who encouraged her to go to his speech in the first place. But he had a hold over her, and I had no idea how strong." He tore the leaf off the rubber plant and crushed it in his fingers.

She sat quietly, but her mind raced to make connections, to understand what he was telling her.

"I found the notes after she'd run off. She'd been corresponding with Allwood." He scooped up his coffee mug and dropped it into the sink. "God, why didn't I stop her?" White knuckled hands gripped the porcelain edge.

Charlie joined him in the kitchen, set her mug in the sink next to his, and settled a hand on his back. "She was a grown woman. She could make up her own mind."

"But I'm her brother." He shrugged off her touch. "I should've kept her safe from that madman."

"You couldn't have known—" Her hand hung in the air. How could she comfort him? Bring peace to his tortured mind?

"Yes, I could have, Charlie." He whipped open the dishwasher and flung both mugs into it, slammed it shut, and then whirled to face her. "I was her older brother. I was supposed to protect her, keep her safe, and I utterly failed."

"Risa." Her breath hitched in her throat. "That's your sister's name?"

"Yes." He scrubbed a hand over his face, and his eyebrows gathered in. "Now you understand why I needed to know who wrote that manuscript. Why I suspected...but couldn't reveal...I thought it might be her. Dreaded it might be her." He squeezed his eyes shut. "I've lost her, Charlie. She was trapped in time, and I lost her. My only sister, dead centuries ago."

And Charlie's work on the Voynich manuscript had been the thing allowing him to piece it together. No wonder he had so much interest in her work. No wonder his actions and words flashed hot and cold. He'd known all this time NCIS-A was seeking out time machines, not alien spaceships. And every one that landed, each pod they'd discovered, he imagined his sister could be in it. Even the one that had exploded in Idaho.

My God. How horrific.

"Is that how you ended up in this time, Angel?" If only he would look at her. "Were you trying to find your sister?"

"I had to stop them, Charlie, don't you see?" He backed away from her. "The Genesis Project. Not only were they breaking the laws of nature, they had stolen my sister away with their lies. With Allwood's lies. He lured her away with promises—"

She furrowed her brow. "Did she fall in love with him?"

After putting the coffee filters away, he slammed the cupboard door. "That wasn't love. Allwood used her. He wanted her mind, her intelligence."

"Oh?" She needed to tread carefully.

"My sister, although raised in the simple lifestyle of our village, had a mind for science and mathematics." He leaned against the counter, and his tense body relaxed as he remembered happier times.

"I thought everything had been lost centuries before," she prompted. A young woman with an interest in science and math, but living an agrarian life? Impressive. "She must've been very bright."

He nodded, and a faint smile played across his lips. "My sister—she was unlike any other child in our village. She thrived on learning. Yes, most knowledge had been lost, but the basics of education: reading, writing, math. Those remained. We still had schools and learning. While most girls cared for the animals and worked in the kitchens, my sister grew experiments in the barn." His eyes brightened at the memories. "My father indulged her because he loved his only daughter. Growing weird mushrooms or strange bacteria or whatever she was interested in."

If only Charlie could've met his sister. What a fascinating woman she must have been.

He swept his arm, gesturing at the multitude of flora that filled his apartment. "The plants you see everywhere? Why do I have them? They remind me of her. Her bedroom used to be full of plants and vines and shrubs. Foundations for many of her experiments." He leaned in to smell a purple orchid that sat on the edge of the counter. "I thought, by having these around me, I'd miss her less. I'd be able to hold on to her somehow. I really believed one day I would find her. But your translations—"

"I'm sorry, Angel." She swallowed the lump in her throat. Why did she push him for these painful details? "I didn't know—"

"How could you know? I couldn't tell anyone where I came from. Why I was here. I couldn't ask questions about anything. I had to figure it out and quickly. You have no idea how confusing it was for me when I arrived."

Charlie studied him from the opposite side of the kitchen. How strange was it for him to arrive in their time with no friends, no family, no information? She had so many questions.

"So Risa, she ran off to work for Allwood?"

"He lured her away. He was dishonest and stole her from us." He crossed his arms and a dark look took over his face. "Who knows what he did to her once she fell into his hands."

"Do you think he did any experiments on her?" she asked as gently as she could. "Any of those genetic experiments?"

His brow wrinkled. "He played into her self-doubts about her intelligence, her physical characteristics, and he promised her just about anything to make sure he had what he needed to pursue the plans of the Genesis Project. Which went much further than anyone knew."

"Was there any attempt to stop him?"

"We tried." He stared at the floor, and his shoulders slumped. "I joined up with a team to stop him. When we felt things had gone too far. He had to be purged. They all had to be purged...every single one of his followers." He spat out the last sentence.

"Including your sister?"

Angel didn't answer her. He scrubbed a hand over his face as he distanced himself from her and sat at the small table beyond the island.

As Charlie stood in Angel's kitchen, surrounded by plants, listening to his story, pieces of the puzzle came together. "Armas could be your nephew."

Spots of color entered his cheeks. "No."

"Why would you say that?"

He raised his voice. "Impossible."

"I think you have to consider the possibility—" Why would Angel be so negative toward the idea? Armas, who had no one, could possibly have someone. An uncle. Angel could be his uncle.

"Stop, Charlie." He held his head in his hands. "Stop, please."

"I'm sorry, Angel." In a fluid motion, she rounded the island and knelt at his feet. She'd have to keep these kinds of thoughts to herself for the time being. It was all too hurtful for him. "Everything you told me? It's a lot to comprehend." The two of them alone couldn't tackle the situation revealed by his story. What if they included someone on the team? "We need to share this with Commander Orr. He could help you."

"No." He lifted his head and looked her in the eye.

"But why not?" Her brows came together.

"You think this was easy for me?" He clasped her hand in his. "To tell you the truth of who I am?"

"Of course not." She pulled her hand free and sat in the empty chair at the table.

"You are the first living soul I have told since I arrived here." His dark gaze burned into her. "Just you. And there's a reason for that."

"You have to trust someone else besides me, Angel." Why couldn't he see how helpless she was? Having all of this knowledge and then having no real way to do anything? It gnawed at her. "I don't have any power. Orr could provide all kinds of resources—"

"If I trusted Orr, I would've told him all of this months ago. I have to be careful, Charlie. If the wrong person found out I was from the future, that I traveled in a pod—"

Any scenario she ran through her mind ended badly.

She nodded. "You're right. I'd never see you again, would I?"

"I doubt it. I'd be locked away and prodded and poked. Turned into a living specimen—a freak from the future. No one can know, Charlie. Only you."

Under the table, she touched his knee. "I want to help."

"I know you do." He gripped her hand. "Would you find it odd to know that I was working on the translations myself? Before I came to this time?"

"The manuscript?"

"No, the manuscript was a new discovery to me and likely lost to time—my future time, that is." He played with her fingers. "The Genesis Project learned to hide their actions in coded documents. We still aren't sure who created the code, but it began to appear in correspondence we intercepted. A way for Allwood to hide his true intentions, the true goals of his organization."

The writing wasn't hundreds of years old, it was a futuristic code carried to the fifteenth century. "And your sister took it with her to the past." Her mind opened and processed the new information like a hungry blue jay cracking into a peanut.

"Yes."

"Were you able to decipher any of it?"

A faint smile played at his lips. "I thought I made some headway, but unlike you I don't have a degree in linguistics."

"I never finished my degree."

"Charlie, you are so unaware of your capabilities." His gaze grew heated. "That's one of the things that drew me to you—so talented, so intelligent, but you hide it behind this façade of innocence."

For a moment she wanted to return to the night before, when she knew nothing about Angel's connection to the pods and time travel. Things had been so much simpler when they were together without all of these complex and troubling details. Her mind was overwhelmed with new data.

With one final squeeze of her hand, he sighed. "I'm tired, Charlie. So tired." Then he tugged her toward him. "Would you stay here with me tonight? I've been alone for so long—"

Without hesitation, she slid from her chair to his lap. How could she resist? "And those other women, Stormy told me about?"

He wrapped an arm around her waist. "I hate to admit that I followed my baser instincts. When you've spent years sharing yourself with no one—living in isolation among crowds—you'll do anything to grab a few minutes of normalcy. Pretend normalcy, but normalcy nonetheless. And those—connections—let me forget for a little while where I was, when I was."

She bent her head to touch his. How awful it would be to live without roots, without connections, without hope. A stranger transported to the past who had nothing. How did he do it? How did he survive?

"I never thought I could have something like this, Charlie."

Their lips met in a fiery kiss. As if the very act of revealing himself to her shed invisible barriers between them. Charlie wrapped her arms around his neck. Angel rose, lifting her in his arms, and headed toward his bedroom.

"I'll stay," Charlie whispered.

CHAPTER 14

Minot Air Force Base, North Dakota

LTJG COLE KELLERMAN powered down the iPad that had kept him entertained for most of the flight from Andrews Air Force Base and switched on his cell phone.

He opened his encrypted texting app to type in a message:

We've landed. Will make contact soon.

The C-17 taxied to the hangar where they'd deplane. Although night had settled, at least it wasn't raining this trip. Besides picking up the body, he had some investigative work to do, and it would make it much easier to conduct in dry conditions.

"Pretty rough landing, eh?" A middle-aged representative, whose name Kellerman had forgotten promptly upon introduction, had wandered down the aisle. "But I'll guess you do a lot of these jump flights."

Why did people assume he wanted to have banal conversations? These politicians were really something else. He'd chosen the second to last row in the dozen or so rows of seats for a reason. Too many words tired him out.

"Yes, sir." Kellerman's Officer Candidate School training kicked in. Traveling in uniform on these flights, though required, annoyed the crap out of him. Every Tom, Dick, and Harry from DC who wanted a free flight shared the space and forced him to socialize so they could pretend they cared about those who served. The less said, the better.

"I'd rather be landing in North Dakota in August than in January." The politician smiled the fake smile that probably won him his seat. "But I'll bet you're a tough kid."

"Yes, sir." Kellerman stared at the front of the fuselage willing the door to spring open to make his escape.

His phone blinged.

Shit.

What bad timing for a text reply. He wished he were somewhere more private.

The older man's eyebrows shot up. "Right, we can switch out of airplane mode." He fumbled for the inner pocket of his gray suit jacket. "I'm waiting to find out how the vote went this afternoon. I had to catch this flight for a townhall in Bismarck tomorrow morning, so I couldn't stick around to find out the end result."

Kellerman nodded dumbly. His thumb itched to unlock his phone.

"Excuse me, Lieutenant." The representative's gaze focused on his phone screen. "I have a few voicemails I need to listen to before I head to the hotel." With a sigh, he held it to his ear and headed back to his seat near the front of the fuselage.

Thank God.

Need those samples ASAP.

Kellerman replied in the affirmative.

Nothing new added to his list of tasks. Good.

As he waited for the door to open, he absentmindedly scrolled through his photos. Pausing on one, he expanded it with his fore-finger and thumb for a close up view. Cutter and Demarco sitting at a bus stop.

Strange to see them casually chatting after hours when they seemed to constantly be at odds. What was up? He'd made it his business to keep tabs on his co-workers. Since Cutter had arrived, the power balance in the office had changed. Any attempts at friend-liness with the new recruit hadn't worked out well.

Demarco, typically cold and standoffish, had changed his tune when Cutter entered the picture. Why?

He scrolled through the series of photos of the same scene. If that drunk idiot hadn't stumbled across his hiding place behind the bushes near the barracks, he would've maybe uncovered more about their interaction. Instead, he had to scramble around the corner to remain unseen, losing his view of the bench.

Were they discussing work outside of the SCIF?

Cutter was fresh out of language school. Usually that meant a stickler for the rules. NCIS hammered the fear of God into newbies after granting them a Top Secret clearance. And Stick-Up-His-Ass Demarco? That didn't jibe.

The exit door opened with a whoosh. Passengers worked their way forward.

Kellerman slipped his phone and iPad into his military-issue duffel bag. He'd have to return to those photos and his thoughts later. Right now, he had a contact to meet and a job to do. Two jobs, actually.

Thank God Orr trusted him enough to not ask too many ques-tions. With more people to keep track of, increased information to parse through, it grew harder and harder to stick to his orders.

As he exited the plane, he scanned the dark runway next to the hangar. A limo waited for the representative and his cronies, who'd nabbed seats as well—all courtesy of the US taxpayer. A couple of airmen disappeared into the night, probably returning to their home base after some sort of TDY travel. Off to the left of the limo stood a dark figure: his contact.

Kellerman headed straight past the limo. No time to waste. He needed to return to the office as soon as possible to keep tabs on anything else that might be revealed in his absence.

His thoughts skipped to the boy.

What to make of him? Maybe Dr. Stern's test would uncover something he could share. Was it a link? Or merely a distraction from the goal?

A solidly built airman in her late 20s with dark hair stuffed neatly under her flight cap saluted Kellerman. "Welcome, Lieutenant."

He returned her salute and read off her nametag, "Thank you, Airman Fletcher."

"Sir." Fletcher handed him a manila folder. "These are the documents you requested for the body transfer. It's late, so I'm to drive you to your quarters for the evening. Tomorrow I'll accompany you to the site where the body was discovered."

He took the folder, and she hefted his duffel bag. Although he wanted to protest, the muscular airman carried it without much effort.

They walked side by side to a white sedan parked on the west side of the hangar. A single light affixed over a door lit up the parking area. A host of moths fluttered around the yellow bulb.

"My intentions are to return to Andrews Tuesday. I've heard there's a flight scheduled."

Fletcher set the bag on the pavement by the trunk, then opened the rear door on the passenger's side of the vehicle, as if Kellerman were a dignitary who required a chauffeur. Laughable. He was reminded daily at the office that Commander Orr outranked him by several steps.

"I'll sit up here if you don't mind." He chose the front seat and skirted around the young airman.

Even five years into his life as a Navy officer, he had not adjusted to the privileges of rank. Probably because every place he'd been assigned involved combining forces with civilians and other branches. At some point, it all became a wash and distinct rank differences grew foggy. His degree and intelligence had vaulted him ahead of his peers, which had been recognized by his civilian boss at Area 51.

"Of course, sir." A strong wind kicked up, and Fletcher adjusted the collar of her shirt, which had flipped up. She took position next to the passenger door.

"I think I can manage." Kellerman pulled the door closed without assistance.

The airman scurried behind the car, opened the trunk, and made short work of his bag. The wind gusted again, and she pressed her flight cap to her head. She slid into the driver's seat with hands noticeably trembling.

"Let's forget about rank in here, okay? We have to work together for the next day or two. I need someone who can do as I ask without any questions and keep me on a schedule so I don't miss the flight back."

"Yes, sir." She took a deep breath and let it out before starting the car and backing up. "I can do that, sir."

As she drove away from the hangar, he took the opportunity to ask a few questions. "First escort assignment?"

"Yes, sir." Sweat beaded her brow.

No matter how much he wanted her to relax, she only seemed to grow more nervous with each passing minute.

"You'll do fine. Mostly driving duty."

"What about the body, sir?"

He confined a laugh to a snort. "Never helped transport a corpse before?"

When he said the word 'corpse' her lips pressed into a straight line and, if it weren't so dark in the vehicle, he guessed her face turned a few shades paler.

"No, sir."

"If it makes you feel any better, I haven't done it either." Whatever it took to calm her nerves. Did she really need to know the truth? "We'll figure it out together."

"But collecting samples, sir." She followed a long, straight road past a chain link fence topped with three rows of barbed wire.

"You only need to hand me the vials and labels. I can do the rest."

"Okay, okay." She took a few deep breaths. "As long as I don't have to look at it—him—again." The airman slid a quick glance his way.

"Oh." So she wasn't quite as uninvolved as he'd been told. The text he'd received earlier in the day alluded to an assistant who wouldn't ask questions and wouldn't have a clue as to his purpose. "I didn't realize you were part of the recovery crew."

She nodded and turned the vehicle toward a collection of buildings opposite the main runway. "I was on watch yesterday when the call came in from Devils Lake. Me and Airman Quintana. The captain on duty assigned me to the crew. Quintana stayed behind." The car's headlights lit up the sign for the Visiting Officer's Quarters. "He owes me," she muttered under her breath.

Quintana and an unnamed captain also involved? He made a mental note to find out the officer's name. Just in case.

"They're expecting you inside, sir. I'll retrieve your bag." She reached for the door handle.

"Pop the trunk. I can handle my own bag, Airman."

As the young woman pulled a lever near her knee to open it, Kellerman thought ahead to the tasks he needed to accomplish tomorrow. Fletcher was eager to please, which should help in collecting two identical sets of samples. One for NCIS-A and Dr. Stern's lab, and one for the professor.

———

In the morgue exam room of the base hospital Kellerman stood over a zipped body bag.

Fletcher's face had turned the color of an unripe banana, and she white knuckled the edge of the gurney.

"Are you going to be sick, Airman?" The lieutenant pushed his glasses up his nose with a nitrile-gloved finger.

"No, sir." She gulped while staring at the unopened bag. "Can I get a drink of water?" Her gaze wandered to a sink along one wall with a stack of paper cups next to it.

"Go for it." The young lieutenant suppressed a grin. He could manage the samples alone if he had to. Why was she selected as his assistant anyway? "What's your connection to the professor?"

Before answering, she filled a cup with water and drank half of it. "Groom Lake."

"I don't remember seeing you there." Although he didn't have the best memory for faces, he had been stationed at Area 51 almost three years.

She crunched her cup into a ball and tossed it in the garbage can next to the door. "Well, I don't remember you."

"Touché." He chuckled. "Feeling better now? I could do this myself, but it would go a lot faster if you could label the vials. Start by adding today's date."

He opened up the hard case he'd traveled with and handed her a permanent marker and a sheet of labels.

The airman pawed through the case of supplies. "How many vials do you need? I still have to drive you out to the scene before it gets too late."

"In a hurry?" This far north summer days were long, and he'd been promised assistance for all data collection—including gathering samples at the scene.

With bent head, she filled out each label in perfect script. "Since they found the body, they've been closing the gate early at Camp Grafton." She held up the sheet with the first row completed. "How's this?"

"Perfect. I'll call out the rest of the label as I collect the sample. You hold it for me while I add the material."

Did her face pale again at the word 'material'?

"Yes, sir."

Kellerman unzipped the body bag. The smell of decomposition filled his nostrils, which immediately turned his stomach. The body had been outside for a week after all. What else did he expect? He raised his arm and pressed it up against his nose.

Fletcher gagged.

He swallowed the bile that bubbled up in his throat. "First vial: blood, head wound." He swabbed at the congealed blood around a gaping wound on the corpse's scalp. Probably the killing blow.

"Vial, please."

Fletcher scrambled to complete the label, stick it to the vial, and hold it for Kellerman to add the sample collected on the end of a cotton swab.

Dr. Stern had given him a crash course in evidence collection a few months back when he'd first arrived at NCIS-A. Such a small team needed cross training in other work. Who knew he'd have to put it to use so quickly?

To encounter a pod traveler's body had been a hope when he'd received his new orders. The professor had been pleased his application to join the team had been accepted. A glowing reference from his commanding officer probably helped. But Kellerman had been a steadfast believer in the professor's pursuits. He stood behind his goals and wanted to support them in any way he could.

No need for Commander Orr to know he'd been sending samples back to Nevada, too. Cutter had almost caught him snatching a few samples out of the bus last week on their trip to

North Dakota. After that incident, he realized he'd grown a little sloppy.

But what did it hurt? Different agencies withheld classified information from each other all the time. Just because one small office had its own mission and its own compartmented source of information, didn't mean another office for another agency didn't pursue a similar line of information. Kellerman had clearance for both, so no conflict in his mind.

He continued his sample collection and, after thirty minutes, the smell no longer bothered him.

"Are we almost done, sir?" Fletcher had dutifully labeled and handed him vials, capping them off once the evidence had been collected and placing them carefully in the case.

"I think this is the last one." With a pair of tweezers, he had removed skin samples from around the head wound and collected hair samples. He hadn't received specific orders about what to collect, so he made an educated guess: blood, hair, skin. He'd also found some lingering green goo under the man's fingernails. With careful precision, he scraped the goo with an orange stick in his case and added it to the samples. The professor would be most interested in that vial.

He surveyed the strange figure in the body bag one last time and unzipped it further to expose it in its entirety. The bizarre foot deformation fascinated him. If this was the person who'd attacked him and the Chief, he sure moved quickly on those awkward things.

"What was wrong with him?" Fletcher asked, gaping at the deformed feet.

The lieutenant zipped up the body bag. "Some sort of birth defect."

Fletcher chewed on her lip and processed the answer. "Weird." She scanned the two dozen vials. "Did we collect everything he wanted?"

"I think so." He removed his gloves, being careful to turn them

inside out, and then tossed them in the bin marked 'biohazard infec-
tious waste.' "Why don't we grab some lunch at the chow hall before
the drive out to Devils Lake?"

"You have an appetite after all of that?" Fletcher snapped the
case shut.

"Yeah, I do." Perhaps this kind of work suited him after all.

CHAPTER 15

THE CAUTION TAPE sagged between the branches where it had been strung. Weighted down with rain from a summer storm, it was easy for Kellerman to step over.

"Are you sure it's okay for us to be in here?" The young airman hung back with her hands on her hips.

As the lieutenant surveyed the scene, he noticed small orange flags marking an area on the other side of a fallen log. "I think they found the body over here." He picked his way through sodden leaves, sticks, and mud. "The authorities who were here before us were looking for different things." With a long stick, he poked around the location where the body had been.

Fletcher crept up behind him. "What are we looking for?"

Every few pokes, he lifted the end of the stick and examined it. "Organic material."

"What kind of material?"

His focus sharpened on the tip. "Do you have a flashlight?"

"I think so. Why?" Fletcher dug through the backpack she'd brought with her. It was full of all kinds of useful things besides evidence collection materials from snacks to bottles of water to, hopefully, a flashlight.

"If it's the right material, it should fluoresce in the light."

"Got it." She pulled out the flashlight, triumphant.

"Shine it on the stick."

With a quick flick of her finger, she snapped on the flashlight.

A warm breeze blew through the elms. Even though it was mid-afternoon, the thick canopy of trees above kept the sun from breaking through.

She played the light across the tip of the stick.

It glowed a weak green.

"Wow."

The lieutenant smiled, then snapped his fingers. "I need a vial. Quick."

Fletcher grabbed a handful of glass vials and uncapped one. "Here."

From his pocket, he pulled out a packaged cotton swab. Then he snapped open the wrapper, wiped at the glowing goo, and dropped the swab into the vial. "Perfect."

Fletcher capped it. "How should I label this one, sir?" She'd prepped the vials ahead of time with the blank labels showing only the date.

"Sample 1."

"That's it?"

"That's it." Kellerman focused in on a pile of leaves right next to one of the orange flags. "Hold on, we might get lucky again." He prodded the spot with his stick. "Flashlight?" He lifted the pile with it.

Fletcher played the flashlight across the exposed detritus underneath. More glowing green light. Brighter this time.

"Jackpot!" Kellerman shook a fist. "I hoped we might find some that hadn't been destroyed by the rainstorm."

The airman prepped a few more vials and handed them, in turn, to the lieutenant for him to add the swabs. "Will we need samples for NCIS-A?"

Kellerman popped the last swab into a vial. "Nope. The

commander gave me orders about the body, not these." He gestured at the half dozen vials Fletcher secreted in her backpack. "But he did want photos of the crime scene." He tossed his stick into the woods.

"Didn't we just trample all over the crime scene?" Fletcher looked down at her feet. Orange flags surrounded them.

"The authorities trampled it before we ever got here." The lieutenant took his phone out of his rear pocket. "The light's shit right here." He looked up at the sky blocked out by the branches above them. "Oh, well."

For a few minutes he took snapshots of every flag, the depressed area where the body lay, and, once they'd stepped outside the caution tape, the whole scene.

"Enough?" the airman asked. "They close the gate in thirty."

Kellerman nodded. "The body is more important than these pictures, really."

They headed back. A mile walk back to the duty van should mean they'd squeak out of Camp Grafton with a few minutes to spare.

Fletcher, a mere five-foot-two to Kellerman's towering height, trotted alongside to keep up with his pace. "So did you work with the professor on his project?"

"Yep." Kellerman took purposeful strides down the trail that led to the parking lot.

"Is this green stuff going to help him with it?"

"Yep."

The airman followed a few steps behind him now. "Before I received my orders to Minot, there were rumors flying around about what he was building in the warehouse." She shifted the heavy backpack to her other shoulder.

"People like to gossip."

"Do you know what he's building in there?" She raised her eyebrows. "I never had a chance to go inside. It must be something really amazing."

"Uh-uh."

The parking lot came into view.

"You aren't going to tell me anything are you?" Her mouth flattened into a line.

"What made you think I would?"

"We both have the same clearances," she pointed out.

"Do we?" He stopped abruptly and faced her.

"I couldn't walk into your NCIS-A office. But the professor's work? You think he'd have me help you, if he didn't trust me?"

He crossed his arms and snorted. "If he trusted you that much, wouldn't he have told you about the project in the warehouse?"

She gave an exaggerated sigh.

Fletcher looked over her shoulder toward the scene that now was invisible behind a layer of trees and shrubs. "Wonder who that guy was."

———

On the return trip to DC, Kellerman was glad to see he had the plane mostly to himself. No highbrow DC politicians or lobbyists on this trip.

A pair of airmen sat toward the front—as far away from the cargo area as possible.

They'd seen the gurney roll in with the coffin-like container used to transport the body.

Although it had been on ice since they'd found it on Camp Grafton, the flight back had no refrigerated compartment. The box stamped "Handle With Extreme Care" held the body bag and the remains of the unknown man. Dr. Stern would be meeting him at Andrews to take ownership of everything.

Before the plane took off and they lost their wi-fi signal, Kellerman sent a text:

It's done.

Three dots appeared and flashed across his encrypted texting app indicating a response was incoming.

The plane began to taxi down the runway.

He stared at his phone. With this job complete and the samples acquired, what were his next steps?

I have a new assignment.

He blinked his eyes rapidly. He typed back:

I'm listening.

Kellerman's pulse quickened. To have the trust of someone he admired so much pleased him more than he expected.

The sound of the engines roared in his ears, and the plane accelerated.

He needed an answer.

How he could help? How could he further support the important work being done? He believed in the project now more than ever. And with Cutter on the verge of uncovering the correct formulas from that old manuscript, he knew he could produce results quickly once he returned to the office. In fact, he was itching to be back.

A new text popped up on the screen.

Not the response he had expected.

Shit.

He answered in the affirmative and shut off his phone for the duration of the flight. Over the next several hours, he had a lot to think about.

CHAPTER 16

THE PROFESSOR FINISHED TEXTING and set his phone on his desk. He pinched his bottom lip. Kellerman had come through with the samples despite many obstacles and at great risk to himself. He could trust him with this next request.

He spun his chair around and approached the large window that looked out over the warehouse floor below. From this vantage point, the project he'd obsessed over for more than twenty years sprawled before him. Finally.

Clear plastic sheeting protected the delicate work from the elements. Too much moisture and the material would disintegrate. Too dry and the circuitry wouldn't work properly.

Workers were split among four separate sectors: material recovery, testing, replication, and application. Rather than keep each group separate and in the dark about the ultimate goal, the professor had built the laboratory as an interactive space. Knowing the why of one's work usually produced better results. It had been a hard fought battle with the security folks who loved their regulations and compartmented information. But since he came from outside that world and had brought his knowledge and techniques with him, the military had been eager to please him and keep his work moving forward.

They understood the potential.

The last thing they wanted to do was upset him and tempt him to end his experiment.

Especially now that his team was so close.

He knew this day would come.

He only had to have some patience.

Someone knocked on his office door.

Pressing a button on a small, black remote, the blinds automatically closed over the window, blocking a visitor's view of the warehouse activity.

"Enter." He rolled down his sleeves and buttoned the cuffs.

One of the many flag officers, this one naval, who loved to stop by and pretend he had a hand in his project, crossed the threshold. "Professor, I have a VIP guest on base today. Thought you could give her the grand tour."

Slipping his hands into his pockets, he kept his distance from the Rear Admiral. "A tour?"

The Rear Admiral closed the door and sat in one of the leather armchairs that flanked the desk. "May I?"

Considering he'd already made himself at home, the question was belated. "Be my guest. What kind of tour? You know we're doing delicate work here."

The buttons of the officer's jacket strained against the middle-age man's gut. "You've done tours before."

"For a select few. And those few were in charge of funds that would keep my work afloat." A necessary evil, he'd learned, in the world of military science experiments. "Who is this VIP?"

"Senator Hargraves. She's on a tour of some of the bases out West."

The name meant nothing. Politics were of no interest to him. The only thing that interested him was enough money, enough people, and enough equipment to see the project through. And he was almost there.

"No."

The officer leaned forward with mouth agape. "What do you mean, no? She's a senator. A very important one."

"I don't care."

The Rear Admiral's face turned bright red. "Who do you think pays for that shit down there, Allwood? The federal government. That's goddamn who." He leapt up from his chair. "You will give this woman a tour. She'll be stopping by in the next hour. Either you explain the project to her, or I'll do it."

The professor flexed his fingers. Every fiber of his being wanted to lash out physically at this stupid buffoon of a man. Who was he to command anything? "This is my project. My expertise. You will not bring an unauthorized person into my lab. Perhaps you need to speak with the Base Commander?" He picked up the phone receiver and punched a button.

The officer's nostrils flared and his eyes bugged out. "I will take this up with the Base Commander personally."

The professor hung up the phone. "Be my guest."

After the irate Rear Admiral left, Byron Allwood wondered how much longer he could bully these military officers before they finally followed through on their threats. He sensed he didn't have much time left before he'd lose control. For years they'd seen his work as 'promising' and 'interesting' enough to fund at low levels. But as his work had sped up in recent years, expectations had risen along with the funding.

He couldn't give up now, not when he was so close. Everything depended on his success.

CHAPTER 17

RESTLESS IN HER SLEEP, Charlie rolled over. Her elbow jabbed Angel's prone form.

He groaned and shifted on the mattress.

It had been a fitful night. Not only was she in an unknown bed, her mind wouldn't turn off. After Angel's confession about being from the future—and what the future held for mankind—should she really be so surprised she had trouble sleeping?

Her mind shifted to the manuscript.

She sat alone in an empty library with shelves all around and tables covered in stacks of books. In front of her the Voynich manuscript sat open. She attempted to translate one of its mysterious pages with drawings of plants and instructions. As she stared at the pages, however, the symbols rose into the air and floated in front of her like holograms. They spun faster and faster until they transformed into words in English that she could read.

Her heart sped up.

She reached toward the floating symbols. When her fingers were about to touch them, her leg jolted, and she awoke.

Charlie looked at her watch.

Five in the morning.

She sat up, a strong need to continue her translation work pushing her.

As she slipped out of bed, naked, and picked up her clothes from the floor, Angel mumbled something. She tiptoed to the bathroom.

Turning on the shower, she waited for the water to heat up. She brought up the notes option on her phone and began typing out what she'd seen in her dream.

Despite the lack of sleep, her mind was clear and focused. Somehow she knew she'd be able to read the manuscript with native fluency.

But why now? Was it the pod examples? Was it truly as simple as that?

Angel knocked on the door. "Come back to bed. What are you doing?"

"I'm taking a shower." She stepped under the showerhead and the too-hot spray.

"I figured that part out. Where are you going?"

"Work."

"Orr won't be there for two hours," he reminded her.

"Will you unlock it for me?" Only Orr and Angel had the combination to retrieve the key for the lock on the door.

"Come back to bed, Charlie."

The tone of his voice ran shivers down her spine. "I can't."

"Yes, you can."

She shampooed her hair. "Something clicked. I think I can read the manuscript."

He said nothing.

"I don't need to work on translation anymore. Somehow my mind must've worked it out. I can read it." She rinsed her hair, soaped up her body, and quickly finished showering. "We can find out what your sister wrote, Angel."

Grabbing a towel off the bar, she wrapped it around herself and opened the door.

Steam bled into the hall.

"How is that possible?" Angel's brow furrowed.

"I can read the manuscript. I know I can."

"But how?"

"I don't know. In my dreams something told me I can. Maybe I've internalized things in my subconscious without even realizing." A feeling of weightlessness filled her. "I'm surprised you aren't rushing me over there."

"If what you say is true, what if something in the manuscript exposes me?"

"I don't have to tell anyone else. Not right away. We can decide together."

He hesitated and pressed his lips together.

"I would never risk exposing your secret, Angel. You have to know that."

He crossed his arms. "I know I said I trust you, but understand how hard this is for me. I've hidden my past for so long."

She reached for him. "It will be all right. I promise." Why was he so distrustful of her? He'd shared so much. Why did he put up another wall? "We'll have time in the office alone before anyone else shows up. Now's the time to take advantage of the opportunity."

He closed his eyes and took a deep breath. "You're right."

She brushed a hand up and down his arm. "The manuscript contains everything we need to know about the pods. Maybe it will even tell us what happened to Allwood or more about Armas."

He drew away from her. "Armas."

Why did the boy make him so uncomfortable? Hard to believe he wouldn't be happy to find a connection to his sister—a nephew.

When Charlie looked at him like that, he wanted to tell her everything. By admitting where he came from, the time travel, the

Purists, and the Genesis Project, he'd already risked a lot. But, God, he'd wanted her. Despite all of his attempts to push her away, treat her badly, ignore her—he couldn't fight the attraction any more. It had been worth it to give up some of his secrets if he could have her.

Even now, as she stood a few feet away, wrapped in a towel, he'd confess more if she'd follow him back to the bedroom. Her intelligent gaze penetrated him.

But she wouldn't forgive some of the things he'd done, some of the things he still had to do. His mission was tantamount, and it was the only reason he was stuck in this bizarre time. To protect her, she didn't need to know all the details. Did she?

How could she possibly understand the hatred that burned inside for Allwood? The seething dark side of him that could be brutal when necessary. She didn't need to know that part. Never needed to know. Only he knew the truth of what he'd done, and it would stay that way.

He'd arrived in this time alone, and now the manuscript had proven true what he dreaded—although many had traveled from his time via the pods, not everyone arrived in the same time. His heart hurt thinking about his sister. He'd never contemplated the idea she could have traveled so far back that it would be too late for him to rescue her from Allwood. And the boy? The last time he saw his sister she hadn't looked pregnant.

He shuddered at the possibilities.

Risa.

Why didn't she escape when she had the chance?

CHAPTER 18

Many years in the future...

ANGEL DEMARCO CROUCHED outside the crumbling structure. A leftover chunk of concrete and metal from The Before. The sun set behind the hills, and a chill filled the air.

A lantern flickered on and off in the distance.

The signal he'd been waiting for.

One of their reconnaissance men had tracked a follower of Allwood's from the market to this long abandoned structure. The farming communities shunned the old cities and the remnants of the way people used to live with their odd metal fragments and broken bits and pieces that held no meaning hundreds of years later. The old ways of living had been dangerous. That's what they'd learned. The old ways had caused massive destruction, starvation, sickness. No one in their right mind would want to recreate The Before. It was madness that would end with death.

Everyone knew it.

Why did Allwood think he knew better than the elders of the community? The ones who carried the stories and passed on the community memories of the troubles.

He scrambled low to the ground and headed for a dark doorway half sunken into the ground. The small team had split up in order to enter the rumored test facility from all directions. The Purists wanted no one to escape. The experiments the Genesis Project had been conducting were an abomination. The whole place needed to be burned to the ground, destroyed. And the Genesis Project followers?

His heart ached.

Although Angel had originally joined the strike team after his sister, Risa, had disappeared from the family farm over a year ago, the evidence he'd encountered in that time solidified his hatred of Byron Allwood and his sick experiments.

How could his sweet, innocent sister be drawn to such a person?

Allwood must've tricked her. He had charisma, Angel could admit that much. But he thought Risa was smarter than that.

He needed to find her before the team decimated them all. His fellow Purists didn't believe any of Allwood's followers could be rehabilitated. The knowledge they'd acquired was dangerous. And once someone has learned something, how can one unlearn it? The knowledge must be destroyed, down to the very last convert.

"Go, go, go," a dark figure to his left gave the command to enter. All were in position.

Armed with farm implements and bows and arrows, each member rushed the hide-out. Demarco gripped his scythe, freshly sharpened that morning.

He raced inside, determined to find his sister before any of the others. He couldn't let her die because she had been tricked. She deserved a second chance. And, as her brother, he vowed to protect her despite his loyalty to the Purists.

Strange green lights, strung together by what looked like vines, lit the interior. One of the Genesis Project's contraptions. Their organic circuits and wiring had been built into the structure. The intel had been correct. A Genesis Project lab had been hidden in an ancient ruin.

Distantly, he heard screams and loud thuds. The fighting had begun.

His throat constricted.

He had to find Risa. The others on the team would have no mercy.

"Brother?" a familiar voice said from the shadows.

A rush of adrenaline tingled through his body.

At the appearance of his sister, Angel's thoughts were jumbled. "Risa, come with me." He reached out for her. After almost a year with no contact, no information about his only sibling, he wanted nothing more than to touch her, make sure she was real. "We need to leave this place."

"No." Risa, dark hair loose around her shoulders and wearing a long green gown threaded with silver, stood her ground.

He scraped a hand over his face. "We're about to burn this place to the ground with everyone and everything in it." Couldn't she see it was over? The Genesis Project had been cornered, and it was only a matter of time before Allwood's grip on his followers was broken.

"Why, Angel?" Her features were smooth and expressionless, and her body had an unnatural stillness. "Why would you do that to me?"

Yelling and the clashing of metal on metal echoed from deeper in the structure.

"I'm not doing it to you, I'm doing it for you." How could she not understand why he looked for her? Why he was here now? "Allwood has messed with your head. Convinced you of lies."

"They aren't lies." Her voice waivered, and her gaze shifted to the dark place from which she had emerged.

He gritted his teeth. "Allwood will destroy everything we've built. You've heard the stories your whole life. You want to go back to all of that?"

"Byron isn't a destroyer." Risa stepped from the shadows into the dim green light. Her appearance had changed since he last saw her a year ago. "He's a builder. A healer."

"What has he done to you?" For a split second his breathing suspended. "My God, Risa, did you let him experiment on you?"

His sister flashed a sad smile. "You thought I was so perfect, Angel. You thought I had nothing that needed to be fixed. But you have no idea how I've suffered with my imperfections." She ran a hand down her cheek. "I knew I could be so much more. Byron was right."

"Oh, sister." He wanted to touch her face, to make sure it was still really her. Her brown eyes had turned a milky blue, her face more gaunt and oddly angular. "Why?"

"All of my work on the farm?" she scoffed. "I could only go so far with my ideas. My dreams of what was possible."

The clashing and crashing grew louder. Screams bounced off the crumbling concrete walls.

He glanced down the hall. When would his team appear, demanding Risa be killed for her part in all of this? "We have to leave. I told our parents I wouldn't come back without you."

She took several steps back. "I'm not leaving."

"You'll die here."

Smoke billowed into the space. Tongues of fire licked the edges of a doorway down a distant hall.

Angel's eyes began to sting.

A handful of Allwood's followers, in clothes similar to what Risa wore, ran past.

Angel gripped his scythe.

He coughed and covered his mouth with his arm. "Risa?" Her last opportunity to join him before it was too late

Silence.

His lips pressed together in a grimace. He couldn't leave without her.

A female follower caught sight of him and backed away with a scream.

He'd almost forgotten his purpose. Turning away from his sister, he lofted his scythe in the air. These evil people must be destroyed. All of them. Every last one. Angel slammed the blade into a man's back as he ran past, and he bellowed in pain.

Blood gushed from his wound, and he crumpled to the ground.

Angel swung again and the scythe cut cleanly across another man's neck. More blood.

The dead man's young female companion took several steps backward, her face white even in the dim lighting. Without hesitation Angel spun and caught the woman in her abdomen. Her belly ripped open, and her guts burst out like pus from an infected wound.

Risa covered her mouth, stepped back, and disappeared into the dark where she'd come from.

An older woman appeared in the doorway, noticing the three dead bodies blocking her passage, her eyes became as round as ration coins.

Angel wiped a spatter of blood from his face and regripped the scythe.

The woman saw her opportunity and scrambled away.

The smoke grew thicker. It became harder to breathe. Fewer Allwood followers emerged from the interior.

Blood dripped from his scythe. He surveyed the carnage at his feet. A wave of revulsion, bitter and tainted, interrupted his duty. He blinked and stumbled back. What had he done? Risa never should've been a witness to this.

He stood alone.

Where had Risa gone?

The cries and screams grew louder. His fellow Purists were following through on the plan. It would only be a matter of time before they turned their hatchets and other sharp weapons on his sister.

He had to save her. If she didn't come willingly, he'd have to drag her out of there. He'd promised his parents. He'd made a vow to himself.

Plunging into the hidden doorway after his sister, Angel found himself in a pitch black tunnel that sloped downward. He dug a match out of his pocket and lit it. It threw out minimal light in the space, but it was enough to see.

How did Risa navigate the darkness without any light? Although the tunnel followed a straight path, he could see no evidence of anyone ahead of him. Was she doing it all by feel? Or had she really gotten that far ahead of him in moments? Or was it true Allwood had given his followers enhanced vision?

He'd heard rumors of people with super human abilities. But he'd dismissed them as more of Allwood's lies to recruit more to his cause. All he'd been witness to were the failed experiments who wandered back to town. The people who'd trusted Allwood and ended up catatonic, missing limbs, huge scars on their heads, or worse. Horrific things no human should be subject to. It was wrong. It was disturbing. It was evil.

Why would Risa think she needed to be part of it? The idea disgusted him. That his innocent sister would choose Allwood over her family. Allwood over humanity. Allwood over everything and everyone else.

As he trotted deeper into the tunnel, the smoke cleared. The sounds of battle from the structure above grew fainter and fainter. How large was this place? How far down did it go?

The tunnel abruptly ended at a small alcove. A string of the strange green lights drew him closer. He expected a door, but instead he found an open archway to a massive space. As he passed through it, a strange electric charge ran through him with a sharp, explosive pain.

CHAPTER 19

ANGEL AWOKE in a cage made of some kind of organic material, tough and slimy. Through the bars he scanned the dimly lit interior of the huge space he'd entered at the end of the corridor.

What had happened to him when he'd passed through the archway?

His body still tingled.

Was it a defense weapon of some kind? An alarm he triggered?

At the far end of the vast room, which was nearly twenty feet high and several hundred feet long, sat a series of large, green pods. At least several dozen. All lined up along a track. A group of Genesis Project followers had gathered at the far end of the string. He recognized Risa among them, her dark hair rippling down her back.

"He's awake!" a teenage boy cried out.

Angel had failed to notice he had a guard.

The call caught the attention of a tall man mixed in among the followers.

Byron Allwood.

He stood out among the rest due to his height—at least six-foot-three—and also his physique. His arms were thin and a little too long, his legs the same. With narrow shoulders and a long neck, he appeared taller than he was. He'd shaved his head and even in the dim green lighting, his scalp shone.

"Thank you, Neil." The leader of the Genesis Project said a few more words to the people surrounding him, and then headed toward Angel's cage.

In the background, Risa ignored her brother as if he weren't even there. As if they hadn't even talked only a few minutes earlier. He felt invisible. Was he nothing to her?

His heart hurt.

He and Risa used to be close. Spending every summer day out by the stream, swimming in the pond their father had built, doing chores. Rise together early, go to sleep late. Only a year apart in age, Angel still had shouldered the duty of an older brother to a younger sister. He stood up for her when other children teased her for her quirky habits and strange experiments. He'd protected her when their father wanted her work to end—saying it was a distraction from the farm, from his sister's future as a contributing member of the community.

Angel gripped the bizarre organic bars and seethed at the man who approached him. The man who'd destroyed his family and stolen his sister. He wanted to rip the cage apart with his bare hands. If only he still had his scythe by his side, he'd take great joy in slicing this man in half, his guts spilling out. He'd tear all of these abominations apart. Every single one of them.

They were no longer human. They were no longer the same.

These followers were in a cult of death. A cult of inhuman experiments and unnatural existence.

He couldn't let them get away with it. He couldn't let them continue. It wasn't right. It wasn't moral. It wasn't natural.

A deep cry forced its way out of his throat. If he died here, his sister would be lost forever. He would have failed. For the first time, he would've let his family down.

"You are Risa's brother, no?" Allwood stared down at Angel. A jagged scar ran from the top of his head down past one ear. "She told me why you are here."

Risa glanced across the room at them both and then quickly looked away. One of the pods had opened, and a follower climbed inside.

What was happening here?

"Let me go, Allwood," Angel snarled. "They'll find you down here. You can't get away. You're surrounded. They're burning the place down."

Allwood held his shoulders back and chin high. "I think you'll find out you are mistaken. You should've left while you had the chance. Now I'll have to leave you down here. We can't have you interfering." He smiled a knowing smile.

Angel wanted to wipe it off his face. Rip him to shreds. Punch him over and over and over until he was bloody and senseless. "Let me out. Or are you a coward?"

Risa helped another follower into a different pod. The people lined up and casually entered, as if there was no raid going on above them, no fire, no killing.

"I am the opposite of a coward. You are the coward." Allwood crossed his arms. "You are blind to the benefits of my work and why we must be allowed to continue."

"Today it ends. Up there?" Angel pointed toward the ceiling. "Your research is being destroyed, your followers are being put to death for their crimes."

The tall man arched a brow. "Believe what you want. I don't have time for you. We need to complete our journey, and then there won't be anyone to stop us."

Rage poured out of Angel in waves. He couldn't let this madman get away with his sister.

Allwood shrugged and returned to his flock as they mindlessly climbed into the pods.

"Go ahead." Allwood signaled to two women who stood near a

panel of controls. "We haven't much time before they come looking for their man."

One of the women pushed a glowing green button and the chain of pods moved forward with a lurch. The pod at the far end of the line began to spin, faster and faster and faster.

The neat line of followers watched open-mouthed with unbridled excitement in their eyes, as the pod spun so quickly it turned into a blur of green and motion.

What was happening? What were these mysterious things?

The two women at the panel stepped away and joined the end of the line.

The spinning pod made an explosive sound, like the booming of a cannon, and then shimmered and disappeared altogether.

The followers gasped and then clapped.

Angel felt sick.

What had he witnessed? What sort of experiments had Allwood been conducting?

"Risa's your sister? She's a genius." The young guard, Neil, returned to his post with a tall metal staff in his hand. "She hoped you'd join the Project. You still can, you know."

"What?" Angel barely paid attention to the boy's words as he tested each slimy bar that made up his cage. One of them had to be weaker than the others, didn't it? No way would he let an organic cage made of green slime hold him.

"The machines." Neil relaxed and leaned against a wooden crate next to the cage, not even noticing Angel's actions. "Risa made them."

That caught his attention. "What do you mean, she made them? What are they for?"

Another follower climbed into a pod, and it spun into nothingness. The line grew shorter.

Angel's gut clenched. Something was very wrong here.

"It's our escape plan." The guard poked at the bottom of the cage with his staff. "I thought you knew what she'd been working on before she joined us."

He thought back to the experiments his sister had spent so much time on. She'd never explained to him what she was attempting. He had indulged her and protected her from their father's irritation with her work, because he loved her. Not because he understood what she was doing. He remembered plants of all types in the barn, in her bedroom, and a special pair of glasses with magnifying lenses she'd had the doctor craft for her from discarded eyewear. Oh, and a book in which she kept her notes.

"I don't know anything." He continued testing each bar. Was that one softer and more pliable than the other? "What are these machines?"

The guard stopped poking at the cage. "I probably shouldn't tell you then." He looked up and locked his gaze on Allwood and Risa, who stood close together.

Angel followed the boy's gaze. He ground his teeth together, and a headache pounded at the back of his skull. Probably from all the smoke he'd inhaled upstairs or maybe the electric zap he'd been given. Allwood wouldn't get away with his. Not after everything Angel had sacrificed to track him down, destroy his enclave, and decimate his followers. No way would such a coward escape in some crazy orb and flee for a new community where he'd wreak havoc among innocent, hard-working people.

No.

It had to stop here.

He had to end it.

Without Allwood there to lead, the Genesis Project would quickly fall apart.

Just look at them. The people waiting in line. Their pitiful figures dressed in ridiculous matching outfits. Like a cult. Even if they were worth saving, the Purists could never allow them to mingle with regular human beings. Their DNA had been tainted.

The unknown experiments could cause harm to any children these others—*these abominations*—might produce.

When his gaze landed on his sister, a pain pricked his heart. She, too, was tainted. She, too, had been altered. He couldn't let any more of them escape. Especially Allwood. If he could stop Allwood—kill Allwood—this whole nightmare might end right here.

The guard, enthralled by the accelerating pods that disappeared every few minutes, crept closer to the line.

Angel redoubled his efforts to find a weakness in his green prison. He stretched and pulled at the weakest bars using all of his strength.

Neil leaned his staff against a crate and joined up with a few younger followers who lingered near the back of the line.

Angel had to act quickly.

He grunted as he forced the green goo apart. It stretched into a thinner, lighter green bar. The force he'd put on the material seemed to be weakening it little by little.

The staff slipped from its leaning position, fell to the floor with a clang, and rolled toward the cage.

Angel winced at the sound. Expecting Neil or Allwood or some other follower to notice and see exactly what he was up to. But nobody did. The sound of the spinning pods filled the large space with enough echoing sound that the metallic clang blended in.

Able to extend his arm all the way to his shoulder through the stretched opening he'd created, he reached for the staff. If he could grab it, he could use it as leverage against the green material.

The remaining followers disappeared into the pods.

Distant shouting echoed from the hallway where he'd entered into the space earlier.

His team. They'd found the hidden passage.

If not for the strange alarm system he'd encountered earlier that had immobilized him, the Purists would've had a chance to end the Genesis Project according to plan.

An emptiness filled him. He had to do this alone.

Angel had only moments to escape before Allwood climbed into a pod and disappeared. He reached once more for the staff, managed to grab the very tip, and pulled it into the cage.

Only a few followers remained, and the line of pods had been reduced to a handful.

Angel angled the staff between the bars and leaned his whole body against it. The thick green strands, already weakened by his brute strength, turned light green under the stress of the metal staff. He grunted, exerting even more force on it.

Now only three pods were left and two people: Allwood and Risa.

Angel leaned on the metal staff one last time. The stretched bar snapped apart and created a head-sized opening in the cage. Not large enough.

He chose another bar next to the opening and began the stretching process all over again.

Sweat stung his eyes. His strength was flagging.

In the distance Risa whispered something into Allwood's ear. Allwood smiled and touched the small of her back. The touch of a lover.

The thought made Angel's stomach heave.

He hooked his elbows under the staff and pulled with every fiber in his body.

How could she stand Allwood's hands on her?

Allwood helped her up to one of the few remaining pods.

The bar of the cage exploded in a burst of green goo.

Angel forced his body through the hole. Would it be large enough?

The strange green material stretched to accommodate his shoulders. He landed on the floor with a grunt, staff in hand. Where was his scythe?

The motion caught Allwood's attention. His eyes widened at Angel Demarco's successful escape.

"Risa, wait," Angel yelled. Could she even hear him above the noise of the pod conveyor? He scrambled to his feet and sprinted toward them.

Allwood rushed to load Risa into a pod.

As Angel emerged from the shadows at the edge of the room, he spied his scythe next to a stack of wooden crates. He traded the staff for his sharpened farm implement.

"Stop!" The cry came out of his mouth in an agonized moan. "Don't do it, Risa."

But the door to Risa's pod was already closing.

He caught a final glimpse of her face. She had an empty stare, and her mouth turned down at the corners.

The pod slowly began to spin.

He had only moments to act.

Allwood leaped into his. The door closed.

Angel reached the conveyor and wielded his scythe. Every bit of anger, regret, and sadness surged into his blade. The scythe sliced at Allwood's pod, cutting partway through the gooey green exterior and leaving behind a jagged scar. The tip of his scythe accidentally caught the edge of Risa's swirling pod. It moved so quickly, it was hard to tell if it had been damaged. And, for a fleeting moment, he didn't care.

Allwood must be stopped. Allwood must die. Allwood destroyed his family and now he would pay for it.

Angel regripped the scythe to swing again. One more cut, and he might slice through and reach the psychotic Allwood. End him right then and there.

Risa's pod spun into nothing.

Gone.

In moments.

To where, he did not know.

The very act of it disappearing with his sister inside gutted him. The forward motion of his scythe lost its arc, and the blade bounced off the conveyor throwing out sparks.

Before he could swing for a third time, Allwood's damaged pod continued to spin. It spun so quickly, Angel could no longer see the damage he'd inflicted on it.

His final swipe at it ran through empty air. Allwood's also disappeared.

"No!" Angel tossed away his scythe and bared his teeth. Rage boiled over. He'd missed his opportunity and now both Allwood and his sister were gone.

The last pod in line ratcheted forward. The door opened with a green misty hiss. The dark opening called to him.

It may be the only way to find his sister. They could be on the other side of the earth by now. Far enough away he'd never find them again.

"Demarco!" A member of his team had made it to the doorway. "What is this place? Have you seen Allwood?"

Lost in his anger, Angel ignored the question. He climbed up the steps.

"Demarco!"

Angel entered the dark green maw. The door automatically closed behind him.

The pod slowly began to spin.

CHAPTER 20

CHARLIE'S EYES GLAZED OVER. For the last few days her life had been focused on manuscript translation while they waited for any news about the body and the samples Kellerman brought back from North Dakota. She rubbed her eyes to give them a break

The transition from aliens to time travel had been swift and almost seamless. All attention focused on three things: the manuscript translation, the arrival of any new pods, and the evidence gathered from the pod traveler's body. They had an All Hands meeting in a few minutes to discuss any updates to their assigned areas.

"I heard you were approved for off-base housing."

Charlie opened her eyes. Kellerman hovered near her desk. He'd returned from North Dakota more talkative than normal.

"Yep." She peeked at her coffee mug, noticed it was empty, and frowned. "The paper work was waiting for me last night when I returned to my room. I put a deposit down on a one-bedroom not too far off-base."

"Nice." He tucked his hands in his armpits. "If you need any help moving, let me know."

"Probably will need more help furnishing the place than moving in. But my stuff arrives Saturday, and I can't even remember what the movers packed."

He nodded. "Been there."

"At least I have a mattress, a couch, and a table and chairs."

"You're halfway to fully furnished." He smirked.

"Let's go, folks." Commander Orr clapped his hands. "Meeting time."

"Yes, sir." Charlie popped up. She had a new presentation completed and waiting. She'd had to walk a fine line between doing her duty and protecting Angel.

Demarco appeared in a back hallway that led to a storage area and their file room. He caught Charlie's eye, and her body instantly flushed with the memory of the last night they were together in his apartment.

Be professional, Charlie.

———

Charlie stood at the front of the briefing room, one of her slides projected on the screen behind her. "After Armas's arrival and connecting the dots, my translation work moved more quickly. It became obvious that, yes, we are dealing with time traveling pods."

She clicked to the next slide where she displayed the translation of several pages she'd decoded over the last few days.

Chief Ricard let out a sigh.

His stubbornness knew no bounds. The older enlisted man reluctantly accepted the newest view of the pods.

"Do you have a question, Chief?" Charlie asked.

"I do." He leaned back in his chair, laced his fingers, and slid them behind his neck. "What specifically have you found in the manuscript that says: time machine?"

"I will admit, those specific words do not appear in the text—at least I haven't found them so far. I based my judgment on the drawings, the clues, and the formula."

"What formula?" Commander Orr sat up in his chair.

"It's on my next slide." Charlie clicked to a slide, which was a snapshot of a page she'd translated late yesterday. "Although I don't have a background in science, it was clear to me that this page is some kind of formula for an organic compound. Likely the compound that makes up the pod."

"The formula we've been trying to figure out since this whole project began." Orr rubbed his hands together. "Dr. Stern will want to hear about this."

"I invited her to the meeting, but she declined. I think she's busy with the samples the LT brought back from North Dakota."

Kellerman nodded.

"She needs to be here." Orr leapt to his feet. "Let me give her a call."

"Already here, Commander." Dr. Stern stepped into the conference room. "Did I hear you say something about a formula?" Her dark brown eyes lit up with an interested fire as she took in the slide projected on the screen. "Hm, intriguing. It looks incomplete."

Charlie clicked to the next slide. "Yes, unfortunately this part of the page was either damaged or faded by the sun. I wasn't sure if the formula even followed modern scientific notation." What she didn't say is that she knew this was written by a woman from the future who had learned science completely separate from the modern education system. Was Risa using her own made-up notation? Or did it bear any resemblance to a formula Dr. Stern could understand?

"I really didn't intend to stop by for your meeting." Dr. Stern stepped further into the darkened room. "I have so much work in the lab, but I wanted to grab a few minutes to update you on my preliminary findings." She fixated on the screen. "But I find this incredibly fascinating. Charlie, I should have time near the end of my day to meet with you about this formula. See if we can figure it out together with your translation capabilities and my medical degree."

"Sounds good." A thrill ran through her at the acknowledgement of her latest work being of use to the group and of interest to the doctor.

Demarco flicked his gaze her way.

He looked worried.

Charlie hoped he could read the positive signals she was trying to send his way. She would never reveal what she knew about Risa or about Angel. She'd sworn it. Didn't he trust her to keep his secret?

Dr. Stern took up the podium as Charlie returned to her seat. "I've come across some interesting findings in the early tests I've done on the new samples."

All eyes focused on the doctor as she explained her discovery.

Commander Orr snapped on the lights.

The room transformed into the sterile, government office that surrounded the team every day. The reveal of the manuscript translation and the incredible information within seemed less magic under the harsh fluorescent lighting.

Dr. Stern blinked. "The samples recovered from the body by Cole have been incredibly enlightening. Especially with our new view of the pods. I've found minute cellular level damage that could indicate time travel does not leave the body unharmed."

Charlie sucked in her breath and shifted her gaze to Angel. What kind of damage? This sounded bad.

Angel kept his focus on Dr. Stern and crossed his arms. He was expert at hiding his emotions.

"Have you compared this finding to the samples taken from Armas?" Orr asked as he returned to his seat at the end of the long table.

The doctor nodded. "I see the same damage, which is what led me to this conclusion. Although the child had less noticeable signs of cellular abnormalities, he, too, has experienced the same as our unidentified man."

Charlie's throat thickened. Her attachment to the boy had been so instant and strong. The idea he could have been harmed by a journey he hadn't chosen for himself was hard to comprehend. "Will Armas be all right? Should we contact Stormy? Maybe he should have a more thorough medical exam. The poor thing."

Kellerman, who had taken the seat next to hers, scratched his jaw. "Charlie's right. We should bring him back to the office. Dr. Stern, what would be a sign of damage? And is there risk to the child's life?"

Dr. Stern held up a hand. "I knew this would cause concern. The damage is noticeable, but I don't think in the short-term it's something to be worried about. As I said, Armas had even fewer signs in the samples I reviewed. But it's something to keep in mind as we continue forward. We know other pods have landed. If there were survivors from those pods, this cell-level sign of time travel could come in useful."

Orr cleared his throat. "Could this be a determinative way to perhaps locate others who arrived before our team came into being? We don't know how many pods exist nor how many arrived."

"Could we use DNA data from the federal database as a starting point?" Angel asked. "Then maybe reach out to companies processing customer DNA for family ancestry?" He sat at the edge of his chair, and his back stiffened into a straight line. "We have to find them all. Every single one of them. This could be detrimental to the gene pool."

Charlie bit her lip. Angel's eyes glowed, and his rapid-fire questions were unlike his usual, thoughtful and serious approach. Would the team notice the change?

Dr. Stern held up both hands. "Whoa, wait a minute. I only mentioned similar, traceable damage because it gives us another clue, another piece of evidence that connects them. I wouldn't say that means there is a danger to us if for some reason these time travelers mix into our society. You are taking a few big leaps with your analysis, Agent Demarco."

Angel's gaze shifted from the front of the room to the commander. "Shouldn't we be searching for more of these—people?"

He ground out the last word between his teeth. When his gaze fell on Charlie, she attempted a little shake of her head.

For God's sake, Angel. Stop.

"When do you expect the more detailed DNA analysis from NSA, doctor?" the commander asked.

"Any day now."

"Before we take off on what could be a wild goose chase, Demarco, let's wait to find out what the NSA experts find. We only have so much money in our budget." Orr tapped his pen on the table. "What you're suggesting could end up costing us more than we're willing to spend. It would be like finding a needle in a haystack. As far as we know only a scant few of these pods landed. I want Chief and Kellerman to finish their research into the radar signals first. That would give us a better idea of numbers and how many time travelers are here."

Angel tucked his chin to his chest.

Maybe later Charlie could coax more out of him and give him an outlet for his irritation before someone grew suspicious.

"Besides the cellular evidence," the doctor began. "I also wanted to update you on my findings regarding the cause of death for our North Dakota traveler."

The room settled.

Kellerman's foot jittered against the floor.

"Although the man had a large gash on his head, which led to an assumption about an assailant—"

Although Angel had sworn he did not kill the man, something inside Charlie still wondered about the truth of what happened in the woods.

Dr. Stern continued, "—I believe his death was caused by the violent landing of his pod."

Charlie let out a deliberately quiet exhale. Why did she think the doctor was about to say the man was murdered?

She sneaked a peek at Angel. He stared straight ahead. Not shaken one bit by the news.

An unexpected release of tension made Charlie realize how insecure she had been about Angel's involvement. She shifted in her seat. The one niggling thing in the back of her mind about him had now been removed. While Angel had trusted her so completely that he'd confessed his true origins, she'd been holding back.

No more.

The last shred of suspicion melted away.

"What led you to that conclusion?" Kellerman asked. "When I retrieved the samples, the blow to his head looked pretty severe."

"The organic material you retrieved from the body also was present inside his head wound. The only way that could've happened is with a massive force as the injury was made. I know when we have encountered these pods they appear to be soft and flexible, but to withstand the energy that must be released when these pods travel through time, they also must be incredibly strong." Dr. Stern grasped the podium with both hands. "His wound was more of a crushing injury that cracked open his skull. I'm surprised he managed to escape from the pod after it landed, much less run into the woods and attack both the Lieutenant and the Chief." She lifted an eyebrow. "He must've been impacted by adrenaline and flight-or-fight reflexes. A very strong man despite his genetic abnormalities."

Commander Orr nodded in agreement. "I suppose little Armas is lucky he came out of his pod in one piece."

"Well, the boy's weight made a huge difference in the forces applied," the doctor replied.

"Could it be the restraint came loose?" Charlie asked. "The seat inside the pod was equipped with a restraining device. Almost like a seatbelt." How lucky Armas didn't suffer any injuries when he plummeted into the river.

Dr. Stern weighed this information. "Perhaps."

"I guess I'm glad to know we aren't dealing with a murderer on the loose," Orr said. "That would add another level of complexity to our work. We have a body. We know he traveled from the future. And now we have solid evidence that connects the manuscript to the pods and to the body."

"Correct." The doctor bounced on her toes. "I'd like to return to my work. There is so much more to test...decomposition rates, blood work ups, an x-ray, dental exam." She waved her hand as if clearing away her mental list. "I won't bore you with the details. His clothing was distinctly different from the boy's. So we have that angle, too. Was he also from the past?"

"I didn't consider that." Orr sat up in his chair. "Since the manuscript has been dated, shouldn't we assume any pod came from the same time frame?"

"Not necessarily." Dr. Stern tapped her fingers on the podium. "The clothing analysis and dental exam might tell us a lot more about time differences. We also have no idea who was writing this manuscript and why."

"The formula might tell us something," Kellerman said.

"Right, the formula." Dr. Stern tilted her head to the side. "Charlie, let's chat after this meeting. I'm dying to find out more. Can we discuss it in my lab?"

"Sure. I'll send you the page scans with the notations and then meet you there in ten?"

"Perfect."

Kellerman abruptly stood. His chair making a loud squeak across the floor. "I have work to do."

Commander Orr snapped to attention. "Yes, we all have assignments. I want to know how many pod signatures you can find ASAP."

Kellerman nodded and Chief followed him out the door.

Angel and Charlie met at the far end of the table.

"They don't understand the danger," he whispered.

Danger? From cell damage? From the pods?

He gripped her arm as he walked past.

"What's wrong with him today?" Dr. Stern asked with a smile.

Charlie shook her head. "Nothing. Just the usual Demarco stuff."

"I'm not so sure," the doctor said as Angel exited the room.

CHAPTER 21

DR. STERN, sitting at her desk in her cluttered lab, clicked open the electronic images of the Voynich manuscript pages in question. "To me, this looks like gobbledygook." She expanded the size of one of the images so that the symbols dominated the screen.

Charlie scooted her chair closer to the older woman. "If you open up the text file included with the images, I'll show you what I've come up with so far."

As the doctor navigated to the correct file, Charlie looked up and eyed the stainless steel table covered with a blue sheet. Were body parts under there? Dr. Stern had mentioned the work she'd been doing since Kellerman had returned from his trip. Surely the doctor would need a refrigerated space to keep a body from decomposing?

Her stomach rolled at sight of unidentified lumps and bumps under the sheet. She swallowed to keep the nausea from building and returned her attention to the screen.

Ignore it.

The body must be somewhere else.

Nothing was under the sheet.

Her imagination was working overtime.

Dr. Stern read the translation file, ignorant of the shift in Charlie's demeanor. "This isn't like any formula I would know. I suppose these are elements here." She pointed to clusters of letters connected with lines. "And it does have a similarity to organic chemistry notation, but nothing I recognize. These letters could represent anything, and unless I knew what those letters meant, these sketches don't tell us much."

Charlie clasped her hands in her lap. "I really hoped we'd be able to crack it together."

"Maybe I could run it through a comparison program that might be able to find similarities to known compounds?"

"Would that work?"

"It might." The doctor stared at the translation once more. "Kellerman didn't retrieve any additional organic material with the exception of what I found inside the wound itself, which was a very degraded sample. If you believe this may be a formula for how to create the substance used to create the pods, maybe I can piece it together."

"Do you think so?" A jolt ran through her body at the thought she might help solve the puzzle of the pods. What would Angel think? Would that be a good discovery or a bad one? She couldn't be sure. His sister had transported herself to a much more distant time than he'd found himself in. What if A Group could build its own pod? What if he could be reunited with Risa? Would he take the risk? And where would that leave her?

She bit the inside of her cheek.

"Perhaps. I'll see what I can do and keep the team updated." Dr. Stern minimized the translation page and refocused on the image. "Can you really read this language?"

"Before I came to A Group, I'd spent a lot of time on the manuscript." Charlie briefly closed her eyes to refocus her mind. "I think it maybe took some time to sink into my brain before I could understand it."

"But haven't other linguists and experts been trying to translate this for a couple of centuries?"

"Yes."

Dr. Stern sat back. "Wow. That's pretty amazing. You must have a real knack for this. I should introduce you to some of my friends at the NSA. They're codebreakers of a different kind. They might find your abilities very useful."

"I'm not sure about that." What would her father think if she showed up at his place of work? Embarrassed? His enlisted daughter consorting with his co-workers? "Besides, I like our little team."

Chad had driven them past Fort Meade—the location of the National Security Agency. The size of the building even from the highway had been imposing with an endless sea of reflective windows and fencing all around.

No, such a place would not be for her. She liked the intimacy of A Group's office, the camaraderie with Orr, Stormy, Kellerman, and even the grumpy Chief. Not to mention her budding relationship with Angel.

"Well, if you ever want me to introduce you, I'd be happy to." Dr. Stern spun her chair and turned away from her computer. "I might have mentioned your name. I hope that's okay."

"Oh?" Mentioned her name to whom? "I guess so."

"I was thinking more about your military career. A lot of agencies will be fighting over you once the news breaks. A translator with a clearance and your skill level? Something to think about. You'll be up for a new duty station in a few years. It might be a good idea to mingle and let the intel world know about your capabilities. Better than letting BUPERS send you off to Hawaii and just being another body in a linguist's chair."

Charlie hadn't even thought about her life beyond A Group and the work they were doing. Considering another station, another job, another opportunity with the same level of excitement and satisfaction? Almost hard to believe somewhere else could surpass her current assignment.

"I do appreciate the advice, but for now I'm glad the commander found me."

Dr. Stern nodded. "That's understandable."

Her desk phone rang.

"Hello?"

Charlie stood and strolled past a wall full of paintings. Dr. Stern's version of the Starry Night Owl had been added to the gallery. She smiled at the memory of the paint-and-sip class.

"No, don't take him to the hospital."

The serious tone in the doctor's voice made Charlie turn around.

Dr. Stern's forehead wrinkled. "Bring him here to my lab. We need to know what we're dealing with."

Charlie wrapped her arms around her middle. Something was terribly wrong.

The doctor hung up the phone.

"What happened? Who's coming to the lab?"

"Armas is very sick." The doctor hurried about the room searching in drawers and cupboards for various medical equipment and bottles of unidentifiable medications. "Stormy found him unconscious this morning."

CHAPTER 22

ARMAS, pale and small, lay on a gurney covered with the quilt he'd been wrapped in when he arrived.

Stormy, Commander Orr, and Charlie circled around him while Dr. Stern took the child's blood pressure.

"I found him like this. He sleeps in my son's bunk bed—the top bunk. When I called the kids for breakfast, Armas didn't show." She sniffed and wiped the tears from her eyes. "I knew something was wrong. He eats like a horse." The young mother gave a wan smile.

Charlie curved an arm around her shoulders. "He'll be okay, won't he Dr. Stern?" But why did her stomach drop at the sight of the lifeless boy when he'd arrived? He'd been bright-eyed and curious when she'd seen him last. The child in front of her looked nothing like the little boy she remembered. What was wrong?

"His blood pressure is very low, his heart rate quite high, and his temperature is concerning." The doctor slipped off the blood pressure cuff. "Did you give him anything for the fever?"

Stormy shook her head. "I couldn't wake him. That's when I called Commander Orr." She clutched her purse in a claw-like grip. "Why didn't I think to give him some medicine?"

"How would that be possible if he was unconscious?" Charlie asked. "Bringing him here was the right thing to do."

"I agree," Orr said. "The boy is special and in our care. Until we know more about him, our duty is to keep him safe and keep him outside of the public eye. A hospital or urgent care would've asked too many questions you couldn't answer. You absolutely did the right thing calling me."

Charlie picked up the boy's limp hand and squeezed. Why did she think that might bring Armas to consciousness? "Is there any possibility this could be linked to the cell damage you discovered?"

"Cell damage?" Stormy asked, her eyes red and watery.

In less than a week, the petty officer seemed to have made quite an attachment to Armas.

"Let's not get ahead of ourselves, Petty Officer Cutter," Orr said. "Could be it's just a run-of-the-mill flu or something. Right, doc?"

"Were any of your children ill, Stormy?" Dr. Stern palpated the boy's abdomen. "Even something small like the sniffles?"

"No, nothing like that."

"Did he complain about any pain or feeling sick?"

"He said he had a headache last night, but I thought he was just overly tired."

"Hm." She touched the back of her hand to his cheek. "We need to bring down his fever. Once we do that, I'll feel better and we can do some tests."

"Tests?" Stormy asked.

"See if he has infection." The doctor rushed to the sink and filled a container with water. "Charlie can you go get me some ice from the break room down the hall?"

"Yes." She'd rather be active and doing something useful than merely watch Armas suffer.

"Thanks." She handed Charlie a plastic bag. "Fill this up." Then she opened a cupboard, unfolded a rag, dipped it in the tap water, and laid it across the boy's burning brow.

Charlie dashed for the door and ran down the hall toward a room labeled 'Staff Lounge' near the elevators.

What if Armas couldn't handle modern germs? What if he'd been living in some kind of isolation and had never been exposed to common diseases?

Charlie shook her head. That didn't make sense. Infancy and childhood hundreds of years ago had weeded out the weak and sick. Without inoculations or other modern medicine, children who made it past the first few years of life would have had a very robust immune system. Wouldn't they?

The break room was empty.

She pressed her hand against the lever, and ice dumped into the open plastic bag.

Her mind ran through the possibilities: meningitis? measles? something worse?

When the bag filled, she dashed back to Dr. Stern's office. Near the elevator she ran into a thirty-something soldier in fatigues. Ice spilled out of the bag onto the tile floor

"Hey, watch where you're going," he snapped.

She'd kicked the ice to one side and tossed an apology over her shoulder.

Armas needed her.

She didn't have time to slow down.

When she opened the door, Armas's body arced upward off the gurney.

She stopped short.

What was happening?

"Bring me the ice, Charlie!" Dr. Stern yelled. She held the boy by a wrist and an ankle.

Stormy had thrown her body across his torso. "What's wrong with him? My God. What's wrong?"

"We can't take him to a hospital." Orr held a cell phone limply in his hand and stared at the disturbing scene in front of him.

"We might have to." Dr. Stern's eyes sunk into her head. "I think this might be tetanus."

"Can't we give him medicine?" the commander asked.

"If we don't get him help now, he could die."

The boy's body relaxed.

Stormy wept and stroked Armas's sweaty brow.

Charlie handed over the bag of ice and fainted.

———

"Charlie?"

She heard her name being called from a far distance. Her brain was foggy, muddled. She couldn't remember what happened nor where she was.

"Wake up, Charlie."

Someone cradled her head in their lap.

With a sharp intake of breath, she came to full consciousness. Her eyes snapped open. Angel stared down at her with concern in his eyes.

"Where's Armas?" She struggled to sit up.

"Hey, calm down," he soothed. With a firm grip he held her still. "You gave the commander and the others quite a scare. They asked me to keep an eye on you while they took the boy to Walter Reed."

"We have to go to him." How did she end up on the gurney? How long had she been passed out?

"You need to relax." His hand pressed her down gently. "You fainted."

"I don't faint."

His mouth quirked into a half-smile. "Well, you did, so I guess you do."

His making light of the situation riled her. "There's nothing wrong with me. I'm fine." She shrugged off his hands and swung her legs over the side of the gurney. "But Armas. He's so sick. We can't lose him."

The last thing she remembered was Armas's thin little body wracked in pain.

"Let the hospital and the doctors take care of him." Angel sat back on a stool. "There's nothing you can do."

"How can you say that?" A washcloth slipped off her forehead and onto the tile floor. "You're his uncle."

"Stop it, Charlie." His posture grew rigid. "Slow down and relax for a minute."

Her gaze penetrated him. "You are the only family that boy has in the world. How can you be so callous?"

"I'm not callous." He raised an eyebrow, picked up the fallen washcloth, and set it on the gurney next to her.

"You hate him, don't you?"

With a sigh, Angel straightened up. "I don't hate him."

Had she hit too close to the truth? Any mention of Risa and Byron being lovers, and he shut her down. Maybe it was something too horrible for him to admit. "Do you hate him because you think he might be Byron Allwood's child?"

"Charlie—" He flinched and jerked back.

"Why won't you open up to me?" She rose to her feet and brushed out imaginary wrinkles from her clothes. "You tell me everything else about you, where you came from, you trust me with everything, but not this." As she confronted him about her suspicions, she folded the quilt into a neat square and fluffed the pillow. "Why do you hate an innocent child?"

"I don't owe you an explanation."

"Is that what it is now?" She paused with pillow in hand and turned to face him. "You draw me into your secrets, because you need someone to listen, but when I have questions about what you've told me, I'm just supposed to forget about them?" Using the pillow as a shield, she clutched it to her middle. "Believe you unconditionally with no doubts?"

"Wait, you don't believe me?" He thrust out his chest. "You think I'm making up stories?"

"That's not what I said." How did they go from a passionate night in bed where everything between them was exposed, to this? She'd done nothing but trust him. Why was he holding back?

"You said you have doubts about what I told you. Do think I'm a liar, Charlie?"

"Well, you kept the truth from Commander Orr and others on this team." If he wanted help, why was he so reluctant to ask the very people who could give it?

"I told you why I had to do that. I thought you understood why." His brown gaze clouded. "They'd never leave me alone if they knew where I came from."

"And you think they'll leave Armas alone? He doesn't have anybody to stand up for him, anybody to protect his interests. Don't you think he could end up being poked and prodded the rest of his life?" She imagined Armas, even now, in the hands of the doctors at the hospital. His life depended on their help. What if they discovered the truth? "Everything you fear about yourself could happen to him. And now that he's at Walter Reed all bets are off about A Group keeping that secret."

"I'm not sure what you think I can do." His empty hands spread apart in a pleading gesture.

"We have to protect him." She gripped his hands in hers and squeezed. "We have to keep him safe." At her very core, she knew it to be true. The boy was special.

CHAPTER 23

ANGEL TILTED his head to one side. "Why does it matter so much to you?"

How could she explain the connection she felt between her and Armas? The minute he'd appeared in the doorway of the sinking pod, she'd worried about him, wanted to protect him. A little boy all alone with no one to care about him? Her heart had immediately opened up for the child. A connection maybe no one else would understand.

"He needs us, Angel."

He pulled his hands away and avoided eye contact. "Sorry, but I have my own problems. I don't need a kid to worry about, too."

Would he be mad at her if she gave him a reason? She had to try. "Risa would want you to care for her son."

He clenched his jaw. "We don't know this is Risa's child."

Did he know how obvious it was that he was lying? "The first time you saw him on the lake shore...you knew, didn't you?"

"What?" He widened his eyes.

"Something about him reminds you of Risa." Why couldn't he admit it? "Is it his face? His hair? Why are you so cold to your sister's child?"

"Any child of Allwood's would be an abomination," he spat out between his teeth.

"How can you say that?" She swallowed hard at the admission.

"You want to know why I don't care, why I don't want to have anything to do with that kid?" His eyes, which were normally a warm brown when they were together, hardened into flint. "Because he's tainted. He's not one of us."

A sudden cold hit her core. "What do you mean he's 'not one of us'?"

"Allwood's experiments changed them. They aren't human."

"Of course Armas is human." What was he saying? What sort of lunacy had taken over his mind? "You're crazy."

"I'm not crazy, Charlie." He stood and kicked the stool out of his way. It crashed to the floor and knocked over a trash can.

She flinched.

"I saw my sister before she disappeared into the past. I saw what he'd done to her. She wasn't the same. He'd changed her—physically, mentally." His eyes reddened. "The woman I saw that day was not the same person I'd grown up with. Allwood killed the sister I used to know." His hands clenched into fists. "And this boy? The one you worry so much about? He's just like her—something different, something wrong, something inhuman and impure."

"Impure?" she whispered.

"I don't help *things* like him."

She gasped. How dare he. "Get out."

"What?" He blinked rapidly.

"I can't believe what you're saying about a little boy. An innocent child." She couldn't keep the disgust off her face. He must see it. The horror she felt at his use of the word 'thing.' "Even if he is the product of Allwood's experiments, is it his fault he was born?" Her body temperature rose. "I want you to leave. I'll drive to Walter Reed by myself. I don't need you."

"Charlie, please." He grasped her elbow.

"Let me go." Her whole body shook with emotion. How could he say such awful things?

"You didn't see what I did. You didn't live the horror of what Allwood's people did." A pained expression came across his face. "If you had, you'd be on my side."

"I didn't choose any side, Angel. I only see a little boy who needs someone to make sure he's safe, make sure he's okay. Because nobody else will."

Without glancing back, she burst out of the lab into the hall, tears rolling down her cheeks.

———

"Did you and Dr. Stern figure it out?" Kellerman asked as he hovered outside of Charlie's cubicle. "The formula?"

The young petty officer, focused only on Armas, snatched her purse from her desk and shut down her computer. "Can you drive me to Walter Reed?" Her whole body twitched.

He jerked his head back. "What?"

"Walter Reed. It's about a thirty-minute drive from here. I already looked it up on my phone in the hall." She showed him the map on her cell.

He rubbed his forehead. "Why do you need to go to Walter Reed? What's going on?" Kellerman raised his head and scanned across the desks in the small office. "Where's the commander? And Demarco?"

Charlie forced her arms into her cardigan sweater. Did anyone else notice the chill in the air? "Didn't anyone tell you? Armas is very sick."

"The boy is here?"

"Stormy brought him to the lab, but they've rushed him to the hospital. Dr. Stern thinks it could be tetanus. I guess I never thought about a child from the past being vulnerable in a modern world."

Her vision blurred. Why did she think it would be an easy transition for a boy from the fifteenth century to blend in with the twenty-first?

"Of course I can take you. Let me tell the Chief. We were wrapping up our data project."

"Thanks." She forced a smile. "I really need to buy a car."

Kellerman hesitated. "That's okay. You seem pretty upset. I wouldn't want you driving alone."

"Thanks, Cole."

He smiled warmly. "No problem. I'm glad he has someone so concerned about his well-being." He quirked his lips and stared into the distance, as if remembering something. "I've never been around little kids before, but you seem like a natural."

"You would feel the same if you'd seen him in the pod."

"Did he say anything to you?" He tilted his head to the side.

"What? When he was out on the river?"

"Yeah." He edged closer to her desk. "I know he was speaking mostly Italian. Did he mention anything significant?"

What an odd question for him to ask. "I'm not sure what you're getting at."

He shrugged. "We know he's a time traveler from the past, so I thought maybe you're reanalyzing what he may have told you. People, places. Did he tell you who put him in the pod? Who made it?"

"If I had those answers, you think I'd still be translating the manuscript?" Her head began to ache. "He's just a little boy. He was frightened and alone. He only wanted someone to care for him."

"That makes sense. I was just curious."

Although there was something weird about Kellerman's questions, Charlie shrugged them off. She didn't have time to delve any deeper. Armas needed her. "Can we leave now?" Purse clutched to her side and cover in hand, she met his gaze.

Kellerman cleared his throat. "Right. Yes. The chief." He held up his hands. "Give me two minutes." He dashed for a quiet corner of the office where he and the chief had set up camp to conduct the analysis.

Chief popped up. "The poor kid's sick?" His brow wrinkled.

That was the first sympathetic thing he'd said about Armas. Some progress had been made.

"Yes. He's headed to the hospital. Did you want to come?" Even though she hoped he'd say no, it was only polite to ask.

Chief Ricard tapped a finger on the edge of the cubicle wall. "We're about to wrap up our analysis. I'd like to finish the report for the commander. Demarco and I can handle things here."

Demarco.

Hearing his name caused an uncomfortable feeling in her chest. He could appear in the office at any minute, and she wanted to leave before that happened. Whatever his problem was, she didn't want to hear about his ludicrous suggestions regarding Armas. For whatever inane reason, Angel had condemned the boy merely for his parentage. The thought of it horrified her and made her question her feelings for him. No matter what he'd experienced in a future time, it didn't excuse what he'd said. Not in her mind. An innocent child had nothing to do with the crimes of a future time.

Maybe he was merely emotionally reacting to his feelings about Allwood, which made sense if she were to put herself in Angel's shoes. But a child? What did a child have to do with any of it?

"Charlie?" Kellerman prompted. "I said, are you ready to go?"

"Yes, right." She gave a quick shake of the head. "Let's go."

As they headed out the door together, Angel stepped out of their way.

Charlie's stomach dropped, and she waited for a confrontation.

He merely side-stepped them, his eyes dark hollows in his face.

Was he regretting his words in Dr. Stern's lab?

Kellerman touched her elbow, and she followed him toward the elevators. She'd have to save her questions for later. Armas needed her.

In an open waiting area on one of the many floors of the expansive hospital, Charlie and Kellerman waited on a bench. She was surprised they even managed to find where Armas had been taken. Stormy and Commander Orr weren't answering their texts, and the building was a maze of specialties, patients, rooms, and floors that seemed to go on for days. Huge signs hung over hallways directing military men and women to the correct department. But where was the department for little boys who needed emergency treatment?

"Ask him again." Charlie nudged Kellerman in the side and pointed at the male nurse behind the counter at the emergency department. They'd been waiting for thirty minutes for someone to help them, to no avail. Everything was hidden behind military IDs and regulations. Nobody seemed to know anything about a boy brought in for tetanus. You'd think in this modern age that kind of diagnosis would stick out like a sore thumb, but no, everyone they'd encountered hardly made eye contact or wanted to tell them a thing and even mentioning Commander Orr didn't make the needle move.

"I thought rank was everything. Especially here. Why don't you use it?" Was her voice sharper than normal? Everything that had happened today had set her on edge, and now she was taking it out on Kellerman. She chewed her lip. "I'm sorry. I'm just worried about Armas is all."

"I know." His deep voice soothed her. "You're aware in DC there are probably more generals and admirals than O-2s, right? I'm nobody around here."

Even as he said the words, Charlie looked up and watched a female captain with four gold bars on her shoulder boards walk past. Kellerman was right, high ranking officers were a dime a dozen in one of the most prestigious hospitals in the country. Name dropping wouldn't help them much.

"I'm going to try texting Stormy again." She picked up her cell phone.

"Hey." Kellerman pointed at two figures emerging from a closed door. "There they are."

Commander Orr had his arm around Stormy's shoulders.

Not good.

Charlie's throat constricted.

She and the lieutenant rushed to their co-workers.

Orr had downcast eyes. "It's not good, guys."

"It's all my fault," choked out Stormy. "I should've been keeping a better eye on him."

"The doctor said there was nothing you could've done different-ly," Orr said gently. "He brought the infection with him."

The petty officer shook her head. "I saw the wound on his shoulder when I gave him a bath. It looked bad, but I thought cleaning it and putting on some antibacterial cream would do the trick." She scanned the familiar faces surrounding her. "Like I would do with my kids. I've never...they've never—" Tears welled up in her eyes, and she hid her face in the commander's shoulder.

"I'm sure he'll be fine." Kellerman stood with feet apart and arms crossed.

"Let me take Petty Officer Storm over to the waiting area," Orr said. "She doesn't need to hear the details all over again."

As Orr slowly walked the emotional Stormy to the rows of chairs, Kellerman turned his attention on Charlie.

She gave him a quick update. "I was hoping Dr. Stern had been wrong about the diagnosis." The memory of the little boy's body spasming and wracked with pain haunted her.

"Tetanus." Kellerman stared across the room at Stormy who bowed her head and prayed. "Who gets that anymore?"

"A child from the fifteenth century." Glancing at her distraught co-worker, she feared what Orr might have to say. Could she handle bad news about Armas? The boy without a family? The boy who'd traveled alone through time?

"I'm sure the doctors here can fix him." Despite the confident words, Kellerman's brow wrinkled.

But as Commander Orr rejoined them, the deepening frown on his face suggested a different outcome.

She clasped her hands together, nails digging into her palms. If Armas died, she would never forgive Angel for acting so callously toward his own nephew. Never.

CHAPTER 24

"DR. STERN, ANYTHING NEW?" Commander Orr greeted the doctor as she exited from the exam room entrance.

The usually cheerful and upbeat Dr. Abigail Stern wore a grimace and shook her head.

Charlie blinked back tears.

As the doctor joined them in their tight huddle, she clasped her hands together. "They are doing the best they can right now. They've given him a sedative to control the muscle spasms and an antibiotic to combat the infection. But they've had to intubate him for the time being as his respiratory muscles were affected."

How could it be only days ago Armas was walking and talking and now he was hooked up to all kinds of machinery to keep him alive? "But he'll get better, right?" Charlie had to hold out hope. She couldn't bear to think of the boy never waking again.

Dr. Stern let out a breath. "I won't lie to you, this is a very serious illness. Right now it's hard to tell if he'll be able to pull through. We don't know how long the toxin has been circulating in his blood-stream. There is an anti-toxin treatment available that they'll give him later today, but without knowing how long ago he was exposed, the effectiveness of the treatment may be marginal."

A rapid stream of thoughts ran through Charlie's mind. "How long will he have to be intubated?"

"Most likely? A few weeks. That's how long it might take before he is able to breathe on his own." Dr. Stern's mouth flattened into a line. "If he can make it through the first few days, I think he has a good shot at beating this. But for the next forty-eight to seventy-two hours, I'd say a lot of prayers."

Commander Orr ran a hand through his hair. "Will he be safe here, doc? I mean, the doctors, they asked us some pretty tough questions, and I'm not sure they bought our story."

"I'll stay here twenty-four seven if that's what it takes. Let me keep an eye on him. The staff know I'm a doctor, know I have a clearance. They've been pretty open about sharing treatment options for Armas. I think they trust me. Plus, I'll know what's good news and what's bad news. That way, none of you have to worry." Dr. Stern shifted her gaze to Stormy's bent head in the waiting area. "Can someone take her home and let her know everything will be all right?"

Kellerman lifted a finger. "I can do it."

"Thank you, LT," Orr said. "I can drive Petty Officer Cutter back to the office so we can update the rest of the crew."

Angel.

Charlie's stomach hardened.

Could she bear being in the same office with him? Would the commander notice her change of attitude toward the special agent? Maybe she should share what Angel told her about his own time travel, the probable parentage of Armas, and everything else.

As their group split apart and headed in different directions, the commander's phone blinged. Then Charlie's. Then Kellerman's. Stormy dug her phone out of her purse. Dr. Stern cocked her head to one side and scanned the group.

Oh, God. Not another one.

Orr read the message off his phone. "Lake Havasu. A new radar signature's been detected."

Another pod?

"Andrews then?" At least she wouldn't have to be alone with Angel now. They'd be whisked away to Arizona and be busy with tracking down another pod. This time, with the knowledge of a time traveler being aboard. A fluttery feeling blossomed in her stomach.

Orr nodded. "I'll text the chief and Demarco to let them know we'll head straight there."

"And Stormy?" Charlie glanced at the emotional woman. "Is she really in the right frame of mind?"

Orr took a beat. "Kellerman, can you call her husband? Have him come pick her up. Dr. Stern can keep an eye on her. "Doctor?" He raised an eyebrow.

Dr. Stern turned on her heel and changed direction to head toward the waiting area. "No problem. You three go." She shooed them toward the elevators. "I want my samples this time."

Orr gave a whisper of a smile. "We'll do our best."

"Do we have time to stop at the base motel?" Charlie asked. "My go-bag is in my room."

"Lieutenant." Orr snapped his fingers. "Drive Petty Officer to her room. I'll meet you on the runway."

Kellerman touched Stormy on the shoulder, said something to her, and then caught up to the commander and Charlie.

"Let me run to the head first," the lieutenant said. "Can you wait with Stormy?"

"Sure."

Orr gave a quick nod and left the scene.

As Charlie approached Dr. Stern and Stormy, a dark cloud seemed to hang over both women. Would prayers be enough to save Armas?

CHAPTER 25

KELLERMAN LEFT Charlie with the doctor and Stormy and sought out the closest restroom. After a few tries down the wrong hallway, he stumbled across the men's room, which was located just past an enclosed glass atrium with well-trimmed hedges in the center and carefully arranged pavers. It created an oasis amidst the stark, medicinal feel of the rest of the hospital.

He entered the restroom and scanned the space for occupants.

No one at the urinals.

He bent down and took a peek for any feet under the stall walls.

Empty.

He slipped into the furthest stall, pulled out his phone, and selected his encrypted messaging app.

Lake Havasu. New arrival.

As he waited for a reply, he leaned against the wall. With Armas in the hospital how could he possibly fulfill Allwood's earlier assignment? Maybe this new information would mean updated orders.

He expanded his lungs and took a deep, satisfied breath.

Hard to believe only a few years ago he was dealing with unruly sailors, and his biggest concern had been conducting enlisted uniform inspections and signing off on leave requests. As an officer in the intelligence field, he'd assumed his work life would be exciting and important. But a low-ranking officer in any designation started out doing the crap jobs. The menial management tasks an O-4 thought was beneath him. Mostly paper work. Boring paper work.

But would he ever have believed a few years later he'd be living a double life and working on the most fascinating scientific discovery in modern times?

His luck had improved when he'd been assigned to the professor's office. Something about Allwood's confidence, his energy, excited the newly minted Lieutenant Junior Grade. Allwood didn't take any crap and seemed able to intimidate even the most high-ranking officers on base. It was how the man managed to turn a ridiculous idea—time travel—into a believable reality over the last two decades.

How did he do it? And could Kellerman learn something from him?

His phone buzzed.

A new message.

> Will meet you there.

Wait? What? Never before had the professor wanted to be present at a pod landing. What had changed?

Kellerman quickly pulled up a mapping app to figure out the distance between Groom Lake and Lake Havasu.

Less than a four-hour drive.

Maybe that was the difference? Location? Was Allwood eager to collect samples for himself? Or did he have other intentions, since he'd arrive well before A Group could?

He texted back.

> Got it. What about assignment?

Three dots appeared to indicate Allwood was typing a response.

The restroom door opened, and two men chatted about pre-season football.

> Sounds like delay. There will be another opportunity.

Kellerman closed the app and slipped his phone into his pocket. He flushed the toilet and exited the stall.

The two men, army officers in BDUs, stood side-by-side in front of the urinals continuing their discussion about NFL teams and their favorite players.

Kellerman quickly washed his hands and grabbed for a paper towel.

One of the officers finished, zipped his pants, and joined Kellerman at the sink. "What do you think? Do the Colts have a chance this year?" He jacked a thumb toward his buddy. "This guy thinks it's their year. I think he's crazy."

Kellerman gave the officer a blank stare.

The army officer raised a brow. "Not into sports, I take it?"

He dried his hands with the paper towel. "I have better things to spend my time on."

The other officer joined his friend at the sink and whistled. "Guess we're just a couple of dumb jocks, huh?"

It was then Kellerman noticed they outranked him by a couple of bars. If the professor were here, he'd know how to put these two in their place. Who cared about football when there were so many more interesting things to focus one's brain on?

Heat crept across his cheeks, and he gritted his teeth.

Why couldn't he think of a good comeback?

His phone rang, startling him.

One of the officers snorted a laugh. "Looks like your old lady has you on a short leash. Better pick up before she makes you sleep on the couch."

"H-hello?" Kellerman answered and backed away from the two jerks at the sink.

"Where are you?" Charlie asked. "We need to get going or we won't have time to grab my stuff."

"I'm on my way." He avoided eye contact and exited from the men's room.

The echo of the officers' derisive laughter following him down the hall.

CHAPTER 26

THE C-17 SPED down the runway a few hours after the radar alert.

Charlie, seated next to Kellerman, kept her distance from Angel. She needed time to process her feelings and figure out how to move forward. His view of Armas was completely unacceptable. Disgusting, even. He was not the man she thought she'd come to know. His carefully controlled exterior hid many things. Perhaps her first read of him—arrogant and cold—had been the correct assessment that very first day on the job.

Angel seemed content to sit alone at the rear of the plane, arms crossed, with an empty stare.

Fine.

That suited her.

Ignore her. Ignore the team.

Go ahead and shut yourself off, Angel. Nobody cares.

Should she find time to meet with the commander while on this trip and tell him what Angel had confessed to her? What she'd translated fully in the manuscript? And the fact that the author of the document was none other than Angel's own sister?

Her stomach burned.

Could she betray Angel's trust? Was keeping secrets from her boss worth it? Recent events told her, no, it was not. The truth was more important now. Her feelings no longer would get in the way of her assignment—they never should have. Look what a mess she'd put herself in.

At the soonest opportunity, she'd pull Commander Orr aside and tell him everything she knew. Angel would have to cough up the truth. Not her problem anymore.

Chief Ricard, sitting closer to the front of the cabin, bent over with an old man grunt and picked up a container of mint gum that had slid off his lap. He looked around to see if anyone had heard and locked eyes with Charlie. His ears turned red.

She glanced away.

He still thought her nuts for suggesting the time travel theory. She didn't need another reason for him to dislike her.

As soon as the plane reached altitude and leveled out, the commander stood and walked to the front. "Chief, would you please take a moment to update everyone about your radar research? And thank you to the LT for tag teaming on this one. Incredible data. Just incredible."

Both Charlie and Cole focused their attention on the Chief. Demarco kept his rigid posture and appeared to be lost in his own head.

Ricard popped a square of gum into his mouth and tapped on an iPad. "Sure, sir." He swiped several times and then raised the tablet for everyone to see a chart he'd created. "After several days of compiling data and inputting radar signatures from various sources, I was able to find some surprising information." He pointed at Kellerman. "Thanks, LT, for writing that program, it saved me a ton of time."

"No problem, Chief." The lieutenant pushed up his glasses and leaned forward in his seat.

Charlie forgot about brooding Angel for a moment. How many

pods had arrived? And how many time travelers were roaming the modern world unbeknownst to anyone?

"At first, I was working with the timeline given to me, sir." Ricard directed his words at the commander. "But as more data came in, and the lieutenant's program sorted through the information, I was surprised to see similar radar signatures going back more than ten years."

A shuffling caught Charlie's attention. She snapped her gaze toward the back of the plane. Angel had shifted his body to face forward.

"How many pods?" the special agent asked. His dark eyes snapped with fire. "How many did you find?"

Did Angel know how many time travelers existed? They had never discussed how or why he'd managed to climb inside a pod and travel back in time.

Commander Orr held up a hand. "Let's hold off on the questions for a minute. This is where it gets really interesting."

Chief Ricard swiped and another chart appeared. "By happenstance, the Defense Intelligence Agency sent us thirty years of data instead of the time period we'd asked for. Without the lieutenant's program, I couldn't have parsed through so much in such a short period of time. But I'm glad we were able to because look at what we found." The chief expanded one area of the graph to encompass the nineteen nineties. "We have pod signatures going back more than twenty-five years."

"Twenty-five?" Angel said.

His face was ashen.

Did only Charlie notice the intensity in Angel's voice?

"Yep, let me show you." Chief scanned the plane, gave a satisfied smile, and whisked to the next graphic. "Here's the first instance of the signature in the data I received: nineteen ninety-six." With a finger he drew a red circle around that year. Only a single blip appeared on his chart in the nineties.

Demarco bounced a foot.

No doubt he wanted to interrupt and ask more questions, as did Charlie, but the commander had asked them to wait until the presentation was complete.

"From nineteen ninety-six through the present, I was able to count in excess of thirty pod landings all over the world, with the majority in North America." Ricard swiped to a world map showing each pod landing location marked with a yellow dot. "We've even had several—besides the landing last week—in the DC area." He expanded the view of DC-Virginia-Maryland to reveal more yellow dots, including Armas's pod.

One of those pods must've been Angel.

Charlie's heart beat more rapidly.

Did Angel ever tell her how long ago he'd arrived? Did he know others had landed in the same vicinity?

"The international landings may be difficult to investigate, as some of the locations are in political hot zones or so remote as to make travel nearly impossible. Besides, we all know how quickly the pods deteriorate. A pod that landed years ago? The best we could probably do is question the locals about any atmospheric phenomena on the day in question. But to track down if there are any survivors?" The chief shrugged. "I recommend that we ask for additional data to see if there are any signatures recorded even earlier."

The chief tapped on the screen to shut everything down and returned to his seat.

The commander took his place at the front of the plane. "Thank you, Chief. There is so much more to know about these pods and the people—yes, people—within them. We know that now. These are human beings we are dealing with. From what time period have they traveled? The assumption made at this time is that these time travelers are from the same era as the manuscript. Which should make these people stand out. They wouldn't have an understanding of the modern world. Perhaps this could make our jobs easier as we explore each of the landings."

"We're going to investigate more than thirty landings over twenty-five years?" Kellerman asked. "We only have six people on our team—seven if you count Dr. Stern."

"We count Dr. Stern." Commander Orr folded his arms across his chest. "I have no problem adding more people to the team, if that's what's required. I think what I'd like to do is split up the work. Someone take the recent landings—let's say the last five years. Someone take the middle range, five to ten years ago. And a third person can investigate the oldest cases. There aren't as many of those. A single landing in nineteen ninety-six. A scattered few in the early two thousands. Any volunteers?"

Demarco raised a hand. "I'll take the oldest ones."

Commander Orr raised a brow. "You sure you're ready for the challenge? I know you don't love doing a lot of research."

The special agent gave a curt nod. "Was assuming a lot of it would be interview work, travel, tracking down pre-internet sourcing for the most part."

Of course Angel would want the older cases: there were fewer of them and an absence of online information. Perfect for his background.

"Fine. That works for me," the commander said. "Anyone object?"

Kellerman spoke up next. "I'll take the newest ones. The last five years."

Orr nodded. "You got it." He rubbed his hands together. "Chief, that leaves you with the middle chunk. I want Petty Officer Cutter to focus on her translations. Stormy, when she's feeling better, will log your findings and create a repository on the intranet."

"Commander?" Demarco asked. "One thing I'd like to know: where was that very first landing? The one in nineteen ninety-six?"

Chief Ricard answered without even looking up from his iPad, "Corpus Christi Bay. Near the Naval Air Station."

A slight chill ran through Charlie. Her father had been stationed at NAS Corpus Christi in the nineties. She and her brother had been born at the military hospital there. She kept her eyes in her lap.

What an odd coincidence.

CHAPTER 27

SEVERAL HOURS INTO THE FLIGHT, Charlie approached Orr about her translation work. With nervous energy, she crossed and uncrossed her legs while contemplating her choices. Although she wanted to bring him in on the secrets Demarco had shared with her, what would her boss's perception of her be once he found out she'd withheld vital information from the team? And how would the special agent be viewed once she revealed who he was?

"Sir." Charlie slid into a seat next to her boss. "I'd like to update you on my translations."

Orr had his head down scrolling through texts on his phone. "Better than trying to figure out what's going on back at Walter Reed. Dr. Stern needs to learn how to dumb down what she sends me about Armas and his condition."

She bit her lip. "Does she think he'll pull through?"

"If I'm reading between the lines correctly, I think they've started him on a treatment plan." He flipped his phone upside down and set it in his lap. "But that isn't why you sat down. What new information do you have on your work?" He swept a hand down his uniform slacks to brush off imaginary crumbs.

She took a quick glance at Angel who chatted with the Chief about something—probably the radar data. Her chest grew tight.

Breaking his confidence had not been her intention, but perhaps she'd put too much faith in him and his reasons for hiding the truth.

"I hope you can forgive me, sir."

"Forgive you? For what?"

Charlie cleared her throat. "Agent Demarco divulged to me a personal connection to the pods, which I've kept to myself. I shouldn't have done that."

He scanned her face, and his expression grew serious. "What personal connection?" For a quick moment, his gaze shifted to the special agent. Then, he twisted his body to face Charlie and to turn his back to Angel. "Petty Officer Cutter, I'm sure you understand that if you know anything that would be of value to our office and our investigation, I want to know about it. No matter who is involved; no matter who asked you to keep things a secret. That's not how A Group operates."

"I understand, sir, and it was wrong of me not to say something sooner." Her stomach soured.

"Did he threaten you?"

"What? No." Her palms grew sweaty. "We developed a—" How could she explain this without sounding crude? "—personal relationship outside of work."

Orr raised an eyebrow. "I see."

The confession caused her face to heat. "He confided in me and asked that I not tell anyone." Charlie's gaze settled into her lap. "I didn't want to break that trust. I didn't think—didn't know what he'd tell me had such a close connection to the work we are doing."

Commander Orr tugged at an ear and lowered his voice. "Should we wait for a more private opportunity?"

Chief Ricard walked past them and headed for the small bathroom at the front of the plane right outside the cockpit.

Charlie eyed him as he walked by. Perhaps the commander was right. She wanted to unload the information inside her before it ate her up, but maybe this was not the right place. "Yes. Maybe once we arrive at our hotel?"

He nodded. "Let's do that." Then, he reached out and touched her shoulder briefly. "Thank you for coming forward, Petty Officer. I'm sure that wasn't easy to do as the newest member of our office."

"I also have some updated information on the manuscript translations." The two went hand in hand—Risa and Angel, the past and the future. And she still had questions for Angel. If only she could stomach the thought of continuing their relationship. She could ask those questions. Dig for more answers. Find out exactly why he'd traveled back in time, how he had done it, what his plans were. She straightened her posture.

"Oh?" Commander Orr asked. "Then I look forward to our discussion."

Her thoughts turned to Armas and his suffering. That little boy deserved better in his short life. He deserved safety and love and happiness. His only living relative viewed him as less-than-human, worthy of hatred and scorn. She'd be damned if she'd let someone like Angel interfere with giving the boy a better life.

———

Returning to her seat, Charlie felt a lightness of being that had evaded her ever since she'd joined A Group. She was meshing well with most of the team and finding satisfaction in her work. To build a solid relationship with her boss had transformed her view of her job. Why did she think she only had loyalty to Angel?

She glanced down the aisle.

The special agent had crossed his arms, stretched out his legs, and had fallen asleep. His handsome features relaxed making him appear less intimidating. For a fleeting moment, he reminded her of her father napping on the couch after watching a football game. She'd grown up thinking he was supportive and loving and everything a dad should be, only to find out if she veered off the carefully created path he'd made for her, his love was conditional.

Similar vibes came off of Angel. The dark look he'd had in his eye when he spoke of the Genesis Project followers worried her. It seemed only those of pure, unmanipulated DNA were 'real' humans to him. The thought he could see others, even Armas, as non-human nauseated her.

Was he only involved in A Group to track down these 'abominations,' as he called them, in order to eradicate them? He'd implied as much. And what did that mean for Armas's safety?

When they landed, she needed to keep a watchful eye on Angel's actions. And what better way to do so then slip right back into the role of 'girlfriend'? Could she do it?

What would be the fastest way to find out more about the time travelers? Get close to a time traveler. As of now, the only one they knew of who was alive and well and within their reach was Demarco.

Satisfied with her plan, she picked up the iPad Chief Ricard had issued her for the trip, and navigated to the manuscript file she downloaded to it before they'd left Andrews Air Force Base. Her notes and translations might be classified, but the manuscript was open source and available to all via the internet. No classification needed. Now that she could fluently read and translate the text in her head, her notes and the key she'd built were no longer necessary.

Would anyone on her team believe she could have achieved this level of fluency in two weeks' time? She could maybe convince them some of the ease with which she translated the document was due to her graduate work. However, she knew differently. Something strange had happened when she'd opened up the manuscript and started over with her translations. It was as if a switch had been turned on in her brain allowing her to gulp up the symbols and spit out the meaning. Much like that night in the swimming pool when the symbols had floated in her head, where she could visualize them as if they were words on a white board.

Her high school friends had thought her 'weird' when she spoke of how she could visualize math problems, science experiments, and other academic work without the need to take notes or study very much. The information was locked inside her head and waited to be accessed. That's why foreign language had come so easily to her, especially. Once she'd learned grammar rules for one language, she could easily apply them to another and another. Then, it was only a matter of learning the vocabulary and plugging it in.

The manuscript translation had worked the same. Once she'd figured out the phonemes that made up each word, the rest fell into place somehow. Too hard to explain to someone outside her own mind—but she was used to people not understanding and finding her strange. Even her own father had been shocked at her and her brother's innate abilities in school. Not much effort, but incredible results. Her mother? Not as surprised. Maybe similar traits ran on her mother's side of the family. She'd never really asked.

Charlie scrolled through the manuscript starting on the very first page. One line at a time, she read it slowly but fluently as if she'd known how to read this symbolic code her whole life. Science concepts, bits and pieces of Risa's life in fifteenth century Italy, and even the birth of Armas leapt off the page. It was clear to her now the manuscript wasn't merely a place for Risa to record her experiments, but a place for her to pour out her heart and soul in a world where nobody understood her, where she came from, or what she'd experienced.

Oh, the poor woman.

A person of great intellect and amazing talent banished to a past where educated women were not the norm and had little power or control over their lives. How did she manage to conduct her experiments and produce a working pod that transported her son to a future time? And why would she do so?

She turned the page.

Armas and I must leave this place.

Her gaze focused on the words that followed.

It is too dangerous to remain. I must finish my work.

Charlie touched a finger to that section of the manuscript. All Risa wanted was safety for her son. How could she not want to help this poor young mother with her quest? Two women who cared for Armas, who wanted nothing more than love and safety, separated by centuries.

Yes, Charlie would do anything to save Risa's child—even betray Angel.

THE END

Continued in Revelation, Book 3 in The Genesis Machine Trilogy

Join K.J. Gillenwater's newsletter and receive a free science fiction short story

REVELATION
THE GENESIS MACHINE, BOOK 3

The C-17 touched down at Nellis Air Force Base. Charlie stared out the window at the dry desert that stretched out for miles in all directions ending abruptly at some distant brown mountains. Base housing and a golf course stood out in sharp green contrast against the natural surroundings beyond the base's perimeter.

She'd come to grips with her plan during the last hour of the flight. As soon as they arrived at their hotel, she and Orr had agreed to meet and discuss more about what she'd revealed.

Angel's confessions had made her feel closer to him and stoked her attraction for him. What woman wouldn't feel flattered if a handsome man chose her to be his confidante? But now she realized her mistake in keeping his secrets, the truth bubbled up inside. She needed to unburden herself. The sooner, the better.

Gathering their go-bags and stepping out into the early evening sun, the team exited the plane in silence.

Kellerman shielded his eyes and scanned the runway. "I have a work colleague who'll be meeting up with us."

"Work colleague?" Orr made a face.

"Yes, my old boss. I guess he caught wind of the same radar signal." He hefted his bag onto his opposite shoulder. "I don't see him here. He didn't really give me a lot of information."

Strange.

Charlie didn't know Kellerman kept in touch with his previous office. Wouldn't it be difficult with so many levels of security keeping individual research and information compartmented?

"What?" Orr forcefully tucked his shirt into his jeans. "Who are you talking about? Someone from Area 51?"

"Groom Lake," Kellerman corrected.

"How would they know about our radar signal?"

"It's not really *our* radar signal," Charlie offered.

The Commander shot her a sharp look.

Kellerman shrugged. "I don't know any more than you do, sir. The professor texted that he'd see me once we'd arrived. I didn't know if he meant Nellis or Lake Havasu. I thought I'd better explain before he showed up. Might look weird."

"You bet it looks 'weird.'" Orr's tone turned harsh. "What kind of work were you doing for this professor?"

The team reached a black Ford Excursion. Wordlessly, Angel opened the back and hefted his bag inside. He took the chief's proffered duffel and did the same. Both men remained silent as the conversation continued.

The entire team knew Area 51 research was rumored to include extraterrestrial life and UFOs, but nobody said a thing.

"You know I can't talk about that, sir." Kellerman's face turned red. "I just thought you should know is all. Sorry I even brought it up."

Orr caught the young lieutenants arm before he could head to the back of the vehicle. "This is highly irregular. If I find out you leaked information—"

"I didn't leak anything." A sheen of sweat appeared on Kellerman's brow.

Was he nervous or merely overheated? Although the early September desert heat felt hotter than DC, the faint evening breeze seemed to be reducing the outdoor air temperature.

Orr let go of Kellerman and crossed his arms. "Then you'll introduce me to him tomorrow when we drive out to Lake Havasu. I'll ask him personally what turned him on to our radar signal. Let's see what he has to say."

Kellerman gave a curt nod and loaded his bag into the back of the Excursion.

It would be interesting to see how that played out. Charlie had to admit her own curiosity about Kellerman's former boss.

"Sir, where are we staying tonight?" She'd assumed they'd be heading to Lake Havasu upon landing, but his comment had her wondering.

"Don't get too excited, Petty Officer, but we're booked here in Las Vegas."

"Now that's what I'm talking about," Chief Ricard said as he opened the driver's side door. "Who wants to hang with me at the poker tables?" He pointed a finger at Angel, then Kellerman, noticeably skipping over both her and the commander.

"Calm down, Chief, we're way off the strip." Orr's hackles had settled, and he grinned.

"Vegas is Vegas, sir."

———

Charlie's armpits were sweaty. She had been standing outside Commander Orr's hotel room door for five minutes trying to work up the courage to knock.

Did she really want to tell her boss everything? What if it blew up in her face?

Just as she was about to rap on the door, it flew open.

"Sir!" she choked out.

Commander Orr's eyes widened at the surprise guest. "Petty Officer Cutter. To what do I have the pleasure?"

"Would now be a good time to talk?" After finding her room,

she'd changed into more comfortable clothing—a pair of jeans and a sleeveless top.

The commander opened his door in invitation. "Please, come in."

Although a little uncomfortable being alone in her boss's hotel room, they needed privacy for what she was about to tell him.

"Thanks." She rolled her shoulders to loosen the tightness that had settled there. "I'll try to keep this brief."

"Nonsense. I was only heading out to grab a burger." He closed the door and gestured to a loveseat near the window. "I'm not much of a gambler. Vegas is a bit too gaudy for me."

She sat in the proffered seat. "I know what you mean." On her way through the lobby she'd seen no less than three scantily clad Vegas showgirls wearing large feather headdresses and handing out invitations for a nightly show at a theater down the block. The Chief had grinned, Kellerman's ears had reddened, and Angel hadn't even noticed.

"So you mentioned you had more detail on your translations you wanted to share, along with something about Demarco's connection to the pods?" He sat in an office chair, which he rolled out from under a small desk. "I have to say I was a little surprised when you brought that up." He flashed a quick grin.

"It will make more sense when I explain."

He leaned forward to rest his elbows on his knees. "Please. Explain."

She bit her lip and clasped her hands together. "Special Agent Demarco isn't who you think he is."

The commander's eyebrows shot up.

"I'm not sure if you are aware, but Demarco and I have been--" She cleared her throat.

"Dating?" Orr said. "Yes, I think most of us noticed something had changed between the two of you recently."

Her face heated. Although she thought they'd done a good job of keeping their relationship a secret, clearly that wasn't the case. "Um, yes." She crossed and re-crossed her legs. This was more difficult than she imagined it would be. "As we got to know each other better, he felt comfortable opening up to me. Told me some things about his past."

"Did something happen between you two and now you're hoping I'm going to punish him for some sort of lover's spat?"

"It's not a lover's spat, sir. I wouldn't be here to discuss something so trivial." This wasn't going well. "It's difficult to explain."

"Maybe get to the point." He glanced at his watch.

She was losing him. In a matter of seconds he'd send her back to her room. "Right. The translations, the research, our office." Where had her determination gone? "The whole reason Demarco wanted to join our team in the first place is because he is one of the people you are looking for."

"What do you mean?" The commander looked perplexed.

"He's a time traveler, sir. He told me so."

He leaned back. "You're joking."

"I'm not joking, sir."

"Angel Demarco is from the fifteenth century? This is ridiculous." His cheeks puffed out as he released a big breath.

"No, sir. That's just it. The translations, the work I've done on them, it lines up with Angel's—Demarco's story. Risa, the woman who wrote the manuscript, who is Armas's mother—Risa is his sister. They are both from the future, sir."

"I don't understand." He rubbed at an eyelid.

"It's true." What if he didn't believe her? "He was worried if anyone found out the truth, he'd be turned into a lab rat."

Charlie explained everything she'd learned about Angel, his origins, the Purists and the Genesis Project, the goals of Byron Allwood, and how his sister fit into everything. She then revealed Angel's view of Allwood's followers—even his own nephew—as impure and against the laws of nature. The commander had been quiet and respectful as she threw out the wild details. At any moment, she expected him to laugh and accuse her of playing a joke.

"What else does he know about the pods? Has he told you exactly how he arrived here?" He had a pinched expression. "There are so many questions I want answered."

"If he knows what I told you, I don't know what he'd do. He might disappear. He might act on some of his impulses. I'm worried for Armas. I'm not sure what he has in store for him or any other travelers we night encounter."

"His dislike of tech makes a lot of sense now," Orr mused.

Charlie nodded. Was he slowly coming around to the truth? Would he work with her to keep Angel in check and find out as much as they could about the pods and the people inside them?

"Keep this between you and me for now, Cutter. I need to think through the implications." Orr touched his forehead as if a headache was coming on.

She rose from the loveseat. "What will happen to Demarco?"

"Let me worry about that." The commander ushered her to the door. "Be cautious."

She nodded.

"I'll be the one who decides when and to whom to reveal this information." His hand grasped the doorknob. "Your translation work? No more reporting to the team. We'll keep it between you and me. If you have to share with Demarco, do it. I don't want him suspecting anything. Otherwise, the Chief, the lieutenant, and Petty Officer Storm? Keep them in the dark."

He opened the door.

"Yes, sir." Charlie stepped into the hall.

"Tomorrow at Lake Havasu, let's keep an eye on Demarco. See what he does."

Charlie nodded in agreement, but inside her stomach hardened like a rock.

Continue reading the final book in The Genesis Machine trilogy, Revelation.

ABOUT THE AUTHOR

K. J. Gillenwater has a B.A. in English and Spanish from Valparaiso University and an M.A. in Latin American Studies from University of California, Santa Barbara. She worked as a Russian linguist in the U.S. Navy, spending time at the National Security Agency doing secret things. After six years of service, she ended up as a technical writer in the software industry. She has lived all over the U.S. and currently resides in Wyoming with her family where she runs her own business writing government proposals and squeezes in fiction writing when she can. In the winter she likes to ski and snowshoe; in the summer she likes to garden with her husband and take walks with her dog.

Visit K.J.'s website for more information about her writing, her books, and what's coming next. www.kjgillenwater.com.

If you enjoyed this book, K. J. Gillenwater is the author of multiple books, which are available in print and in eBook format at multiple vendors.

- The Genesis Machine Trilogy: Inception, Decryption, and Revelation
- Revenge Honeymoon
- Illegal
- Aurora's Gold
- The Ninth Curse
- The Little Black Box
- Acapulco Nights

- Blood Moon

Short Stories & Short Story Collections:

- Skyfall
- Nemesis
- The Man in 14C
- Charlie and the Zombie Factory